# "Let me get this straight. I can share a life with you, but not love?"

"Not unless you want a world full of hurt," he replied.

"And that's supposed to induce me to marry you?"

"No. That's supposed to make you think long and hard. Are you in the market for practical, or are you Cinderella waiting for the prince? Fantasy or reality?"

Didn't Chaz realize? He was that prince, their hearts and souls joined on a fateful night nine impossibly long years ago.

"Why don't you kiss me, Chaz, and we'll see whether it's fantasy or reality."

He captured her in his arms, his hands strong and firm on her back. "I intend to see to it that you go into this marriage with your eyes wide open...."

Dear Reader,

I'm a bit sad as I write this letter, because it brings to a close my latest Cinderella Ball story, a collection of stories that have lived in my heart for years, rich with characters who have filled more days than I can count with laughter and happiness. Thank you for allowing me to share their adventures in love with you through the FAIRYTALE WEDDINGS series.

Although these tales all began in the same place, it won't matter if this is the first Cinderella Ball you've attended, or if you've visited every one of them. Each book stands alone. The stories are simply born at the same place—a marriage ball.

So here's one final invitation to attend the Beaumonts' Cinderella Ball, a masked affair this time. Take a break from reality and join the other guests as they dream of romance and love at first sight and stories that can only end happily ever after. Meet a cold, lonely man, Chaz McIntyre, who lost his ability to love long ago, when he lost his Forever Love. And meet Shayne Beaumont, his *Long-Lost Bride*, a woman determined to return love to her husband's life so they can both live happily ever after. See what happens when a masked woman of unusual generosity seduces one stubborn rancher who doesn't "do" Christmas. I hope you'll enjoy this story as much as I enjoyed writing it!

Love,

*Day Leclaire*

# Long-Lost Bride
## Day Leclaire

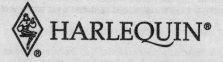

# HARLEQUIN®

TORONTO • NEW YORK • LONDON
AMSTERDAM • PARIS • SYDNEY • HAMBURG
STOCKHOLM • ATHENS • TOKYO • MILAN • MADRID
PRAGUE • WARSAW • BUDAPEST • AUCKLAND

To Frank, my Forever Love

ISBN 0-373-03579-9

LONG-LOST BRIDE

First North American Publication 1999.

Copyright © 1999 by Day Totton Smith.

Visit us at www.romance.net

Printed in U.S.A.

# PROLOGUE

*The Beaumonts—Forever, Nevada*

ELLA Beaumont rolled onto her hip and stared at her husband. A full moon made that job a little easier, burnishing the room in silver and painting a swath of gentle ivory across Rafe's hard-chiseled features. "Are you sure we're doing the right thing, Rafe? Maybe we shouldn't interfere."

"My interference is what put my sister in this situation to begin with. I stayed out of it for the past nine years, hoping against hope that Shayne would find someone. But there's never been anyone else for her. Not one single man who's captured her heart."

"Except McIntyre," Ella said softly.

Rafe nodded. "Except McIntyre."

"How do you know he's not married? How do you know he'll come?"

"I've made it my business to keep a watchful eye on him since I had their marriage annulled."

She took a moment to absorb that before very gently informing her husband, "As much as you might want to, you can't play God."

"I'm not playing at anything." He set his jaw in a manner she recognized all too well. It spoke of rock-solid determination. It also warned that she wouldn't sway him. Not on this point. "I'm attempting to set right a wrong. If it succeeds, Shayne will finally have her happiness."

5

"And if it doesn't?"

Grief silvered his eyes. "Then at least I will have given her the chance I stole all those years ago."

*Lullabye, Colorado*

"You *can't* be serious!"

Doña Isabella inclined her head in a regal fashion, her grip tightening on her gold-tipped cane. "I am quite serious, Señor McIntyre. You knew those were my terms when I contacted you last month. Yet, you have done nothing about implementing them."

"You expect me to find a wife in one short month?" he demanded savagely.

"No." Black eyes flashed above a strongly hooked nose. "I now expect you to find a wife in one short week."

And that said it all. He paced the length of his office, fighting for control. Reining in his temper proved as difficult as reining in a wild stallion bent on freedom. He didn't doubt for a minute that Doña Isabella fully expected him to have a bride on his arm at the end of the allotted seven days. It didn't matter that marriage was the last thing he wanted. It didn't matter that there wasn't a chance in hell that a woman within a hundred miles of his ranch would take him on or that he had nothing to give a wife. All that mattered was that she'd decreed he do as she demanded or she'd refuse to give him the one thing he wanted most in the world.

Forced to admit he'd run out of options, he acted in the only way he could under the circumstances. He shot her a cocky grin. "I don't suppose you have any candidates available?"

Doña Isabella's mouth thinned. Apparently, a sense of humor wasn't a characteristic she openly embraced. "I leave for Mexico in one week, Señor McIntyre. If at that time you've met all my demands, I'll give you what you wish. If not..." She shrugged, her black eyes coldly implacable. "It's your choice."

His grin vanished. "No, madam. It's not," he assured her, just as coldly. "If it was, we wouldn't be having this discussion."

A brief knock sounded and Chaz's foreman, Penny, pushed the office door open a scant inch. No doubt fear of the intimidating Doña kept him from opening it any further. "Hey, boss?"

"I thought I told you not to—"

"Yeah, I know. Sorry about that. But there's a really strange guy out here and I'm afraid if you don't see to it your own self and get him out of here, somebody's like as not to shoot him purely on the principal of the thing."

Damn. "Excuse me," Chaz said to his guest. He received another of the Doña's regal nods and amusement vied with frustration. As though he needed permission from her to run his own household! He swore beneath his breath. Unfortunately, that was precisely the case. For now.

Stepping into the entrance hall, he confronted a sight he thought he'd put behind him nine long years ago. A man stood there, a man who looked about as uncomfortable as a body could. Dressed in white and gold satin, his uniform sported braided nonsense on the shoulders and down the front of his short bolero jacket. Honest-to-goodness lace decorated his womanish shirt and the end of his sleeves. He clutched a gold tray with hands encased in spotless white gloves—hiding sweaty palms, no doubt.

A thick embossed envelope was propped in the center of the tray, the death grip the man had on the flimsy piece of metal suggesting he expected to have to use it to defend himself. Smart fella. Something about fancy duds and a ranch just didn't go together, and all three of them were painfully aware of that fact.

"I'm looking for a Mr. Cassius McIntyre," the man announced.

"It's Chaz. And you found him."

The footman didn't attempt to disguise his relief. "Allow me to present you with a special invitation to the Cinderella Ball." He offered the thick, gold-embossed envelope on the tray.

It was everything Chaz could do to keep from laughing. But he managed. "Didn't apply to the ball."

"No, sir. The application was made in your name."

Chaz's eyes narrowed, the laughter draining right out of him. "Now who do you suppose would have done such a foolhardy thing?"

"I wouldn't know, sir."

"Well, you can take that envelope and—" He broke off, painfully aware of two infuriating facts. First, this just might provide the solution he needed. And second, the people providing that solution were the very last he'd ever wanted to see again. Fate, it would seem, had decided to take another swing at him.

"Go on," Penny encouraged eagerly. "Tell him to shove it where the sun don't shine."

"Get back to work, old man." Of course, his foreman instantly obeyed by digging in his heels and folding his scrawny arms across an equally scrawny chest.

Chaz sighed. "What happens if I refuse the envelope?" he asked Mr. Silk-and-Lace.

"I'm instructed to leave it. What you choose to do with it is your business. But under no circumstances am I to return the envelope to the Beaumonts."

Chaz's gaze sharpened. "The Beaumonts?" The question had more bite than he'd intended. The footman took a hasty step backward, raising the tray like a shield. "Rafe Beaumont?"

"Yes, sir."

"What happened to the Montagues?"

"The elder Montagues have retired. Their daughter, Ella, is now married to Mr. Beaumont, and they host the balls."

"Give me the envelope. Now."

"At once, sir." With a quick nod, the footman extended the tray once again. It trembled notably. The second Chaz took the envelope, the footman turned around and hotfooted it out the front door toward a waiting limo.

"What's in the envelope?" Penny questioned suspiciously.

"An invite."

"What sorta invite?"

"It's for a lot of things." To revisit the past. For revenge. But most importantly, it was an invitation that would allow him to satisfy Doña Isabella's demands.

"Huh?"

"You heard the man, Penny." Chaz fixed his attention on the envelope, sensing the winds of change sweeping across the Rocky Mountains. Dry, harsh winds originating from the unforgiving desert surrounding Forever, Nevada. "It's for a ball. A marriage ball. Meet the woman of your dreams and marry her—all in one night.''

"And you're going to this ball thing the idiot was talking about?'' his foreman asked incredulously.

"Yeah, old man. I am.'' A remote coldness filled the crags of a hard-lived face. "Not only am I going, I'll be bringing back a wife.''

*The Beaumont Residence—La Finca de Esperanza, Milagra, Costa Rica*

Shayne stared up at the starlit Costa Rican sky. The moon hovered overhead, as full and white and beautiful as any she'd seen. She opened her hand and stared at the gold ticket that had arrived by special messenger earlier that day. It glittered gently beneath the moon's softer light. But even so, it had a brilliant flash and fire she remembered well, one that spoke of hope and love…and dreams long lost.

"Why did he send it?'' she asked aloud.

Of course, there was no answer. Not that she expected any. She didn't have any doubt that her brother was behind the gift. Was it a prompt? A suggestion that she get on with her life? She'd done that already. Okay, so she wasn't happily married like Rafe and Ella. Still… She had a satisfying career. She ran the coffee *finca* when her brother was absent. And she was content, if not perfectly happy. What more could she want?

*Chaz McIntyre.*

His name came as easily to mind now as it had nine impossibly long years ago. Where was he? What was he up to? Did he ever think about her and what they'd almost had? Or had he moved on with that part of his life?

For a long time she stood sheathed in white light, the ticket glowing in her palm like a living entity. Finally, she closed her fingers around it and lifted her face to the moon.

"I'll do it. One last time, I'll attend the Cinderella Ball."

The ball would be the key to her future. She'd move forward by stepping into a new life. She'd finally put the past behind her once and for all. And never again would she look back with regret.

# CHAPTER ONE

*To My Long-Lost Bride,*
*I don't know if this will ever reach you.*
*Whether you will ever know how I've searched for*
*you over the past two months—ever since the*
*night we married at the Cinderella Ball. But I*
*have searched.*
*Everywhere.*
*The Montagues won't give me any information,*
*even though I've shown them our marriage li-*
*cense. I spoke to Ella. She's hurting because of*
*your brother, too. It's like you've vanished off the*
*face of the earth. I'm thinking of hiring a private*
*investigator to find you, but I don't know where*
*to tell him to look. All you said was you lived on*
*a coffee plantation. But where? Dammit, it never*
*occurred to me to ask! I thought we'd have all the*
*time in the world to find out the details of our past.*
*Know this, light of my soul.... The one thing*
*that won't vanish is what I feel for you. You are*
*my life and my love, my one star in a dark night*
*sky. Fight for what we had. And come back to me.*
*Until that day, you live in my heart, my Forever*
*Love.*

*The Beaumonts' Cinderella Ball—Forever, Nevada*

CHAZ McIntyre propped a shoulder against the wall as
he waited for the reception line to move forward. What

the *hell* was he doing here? Here, of all places. This had to be the one corner in Hades guaranteed to hold the worst memories of any he'd ever experienced. And yet here he stood, like some sort of fool, begging Rafe Beaumont to stick it to him one last time.

He swore viciously beneath his breath. He'd spent years protecting himself from the sort of hurt Beaumont specialized in doling out. Still, with one unreasonable decree, an arrogant old woman had done the impossible—put him right back where he least wanted to be.

The line inched forward a little farther and he caught a glimpse of the man who'd taken such delight in screwing with his life. Amazing. Nine years had passed and yet the SOB hadn't changed a lick. What about Shayne? he couldn't help wondering. Had she changed? She'd have had to. When he'd last seen her, she'd been a seventeen-year-old child pretending to be an adult. Now she'd be...what? Twenty-six? Almost twenty-seven. Would she be here tonight? Is that why Rafe had sent the ticket?

A coldness seeped deep inside, relentless and all-pervasive, consuming him with comforting familiarity. Shayne didn't matter. Nothing mattered except achieving his goal.

It took another few minutes before he reached the head of the line. Ella Montague stood at Rafe's side. Correction. Ella Beaumont. She'd been a Montague when they'd last met. So Rafe had gained a wife, while robbing Chaz of his. The sheer irony made him bare his teeth in a parody of a smile.

"McIntyre," Rafe greeted him with a stiff nod.

"Beaumont." Chaz caught the wary look in the

older man's eyes and allowed his smile to grow, edging it with animosity. "Fancy meetin' you here."

"You came. I wasn't sure you would."

"Mind telling me why you sent the ticket?"

Rafe hesitated and then inclined his head toward an area where they'd have more privacy. Once they were clear of the reception line, he said, "I thought I owed it to you."

"Now why would you think you owe me anything?" The soft question had an unexpected bite.

A muscle rippled along Rafe's jawline, acknowledging the hit. "You wish me to admit it? Very well. I interfered in your marriage, in your relationship with my sister. Does that satisfy you?"

It should have. But for some infuriating reason, it didn't. He checked his anger, aware it would be a mistake to allow it too much freedom. Once released, it would be near impossible to contain. "You were just protecting your family. I can understand that. I'd probably have done the same thing if I'd found my seventeen-year-old sister shacked up with an older man."

"You weren't shacked up. You were married."

"Well... Not legally." The wrath Chaz had been struggling to control surged to the surface. It shocked him to realize he still reacted with such unchecked fury, even after all these years. "You saw to that, right?"

"She was a vulnerable child! She slipped into the ball when no one was looking. And then she attached herself to the first man to smile at her." Apparently, Chaz wasn't the only one still harboring hard feelings. "What did you expect me to do?"

"I expected you to give us a chance."

"How? Why?" Rafe's voice dropped, the sound

raw with frustration. "I was due to return to Costa Rica. You expected me to leave my seventeen-year-old sister behind with a man she'd known only a few short hours? You were a footloose cowboy without home or roots or goals. What if something had gone wrong? What if she'd needed me?"

"She was my wife, dammit. Did you really think I'd do anything to harm her?"

"How would I know? You admitted you had attended on a whim. You didn't even have a ticket. You simply slipped in through the garden. You could have been anyone. A security check hadn't even been run on you. You were a self-confessed drifter."

That stung. "I was a wrangler."

"Who hadn't remained in any one place for longer than a season. What sort of life is that for a young girl?"

"You weren't willing to give me a chance to make a home with her. You barged into our hotel room, knocked me on my backside without waiting for an explanation and took my wife from me."

"My sister!"

Chaz caught himself in time and exchanged glares with Rafe. This was ridiculous. He refused to get into a slanging match over events nearly a decade old. It wasn't worth it. Besides, he had other business to take care of tonight. "Forget it, Beaumont. It's not important any more."

After a long moment, Rafe nodded in agreement. "Very well. I appreciate your coming."

"I'm sure." Chaz shifted impatiently. He didn't have time for social niceties, particularly those coming years too late. "Now, if you'll excuse me—"

He'd only managed two short steps before Rafe

stopped him in his tracks. "Aren't you even going to ask about her?"

Chaz didn't bother to turn around. "No."

"Then why the hell did you come?"

Ella approached just then, laying a restraining hand on Rafe's arm. "Easy, darling. You weren't going to lose your temper, remember?" She turned her attention to Chaz. "My husband's question is a good one. If you didn't come back to find out about Shayne, why are you here?

He turned. Interesting. Apparently the Beaumonts had a hidden agenda. Now why didn't that come as a surprise? Unable to resist, he slashed at his opponent. "I came for the same reason all your other guests have. To find myself a wife." He cocked an eyebrow. "I assume you don't have any objections?"

Rafe's mouth tightened—a dead giveaway. Apparently, he had plenty of objections, though none he intended to state. "Not a one. I won't bother giving you the usual rundown since this isn't your first visit. I'm sure you remember where to find food and so forth."

"Not to mention the women." He offered a slow, insolent smile. "Think I'll stick to the more enjoyable aspects of your shindig. Food can wait."

"In case you weren't aware, it's a masked ball this time."

"Yeah, I read that. Guess I forgot mine."

Rafe inclined his head as regally as the Doña. "You'll find extra masks on the table behind you. Help yourself."

So stiff. So arrogant. So damned in control of his world and everyone in it. Chaz longed to take some of the stuffing out of his former brother-in-law. But he didn't dare. As much as he resented it, he needed Rafe's help. Or rather, he needed what Rafe's ball so amply provided.... Women.

"Thanks. I'll do that." Chaz glanced at his hostess. "It's been a pleasure, Cinder-girl." Snagging a mask, he headed for the ballroom. And all the while he cursed himself for a fool. An odd warmth sparked close to the inner core of ice that protected him.

He should have let Beaumont tell him about Shayne.

Shayne stood on the balcony looking down at the crowd. This was it. Her last Cinderella Ball. The last time she'd allow herself to remember, to allow regret to overshadow all that life had to offer. To hide from pain and sleep, when she should be living. As this night waned and the sun rose on a new day, she'd confront the future, instead of constantly looking over her shoulder toward the past.

She glanced at the reception line. Her nephew, Donato, had long ago been put to bed and yet there was still a steady stream of visitors arriving, though the crowd had lightened somewhat. Perhaps she should go over and offer to take tickets again. Rafe had insisted she should enjoy herself, but she felt guilty dumping all the work on her brother and sister-in-law.

Studying Rafe, she frowned. Who was he talking to? If she didn't know better, she'd swear he was annoyed. Possibly, more than annoyed. His shoulders were rigid, his hands opening and closing into fists. What in the world had set him off? The crowd shifted and then she saw what had caused him such distress.

Chaz McIntyre stood at the head of the line.

Shock rolled over her like storm-driven waves, threatening to sweep her feet out from under her. From a great distance she heard the urgent clamor of silver-toned chimes and realized she must be trembling, setting off the strings of bells decorating her mask. She gripped the banister to keep from falling and the bells quieted. Dear heavens, how could it be? After all these years, her husband had returned. *Why?* Why now when the time had come to move on? What did he want? Or should she be asking...*who?* As she stood and watched, Chaz walked over to the table holding the spare masks and selected one. Then he plunged into the ballroom.

Understanding struck with as much pain and power as a fist to the chin. Finally, her prayers had been answered. Her husband had come back. The painful irony was... In all likelihood, he hadn't returned for her.

For the first time in years, Shayne acted without thought. Her mask hung from her arm—an elaborate beaded and feathered affair decorated with the tiny bells that announced her slightest movement. It covered most of her face, making it almost impossible to identify her. She slipped it over her head, the bells singing a song of urgency. Crossing to the staircase leading to the ballroom, she lifted the wide skirts of her gold dress and descended the steps, searching the crowd for a tall, well-built man, brown hair highlighted with streaks of sun-bleached gold, dressed in a Western-cut brown tux.

It took her forever to reach the ballroom. Three different people required assistance and she didn't want to abandon them until their needs were met. Finally she reached the dance floor. She spotted Chaz almost immediately, standing to one side, calmly scrutinizing the three women who ringed him—a dainty blonde, a willowy redhead and a sultry brunette. It stopped her dead in her tracks.

What in the world was he up to? He couldn't be here to find a wife. Her pulse picked up. Could he? Slipping close enough to observe, she watched as he swept first one of the women, then another onto the dance floor. He still moved as gracefully as she recalled, his movements sure and powerful.

A man appeared at Shayne's elbow. "Excuse me, would you care to dance?"

"No, thanks," she demurred.

"Please?" He smiled with unexpected charm. "Just one?"

What could it hurt? She'd help a guest and it would give her the opportunity to study Chaz without his noticing. "All right."

"The name's Sotherland." He swung her around in an easy circle. "August Sotherland."

"Hello, Mr. Sotherland. I'm Shayne."

"So you're hoping to get married?"

"No, I'm afraid not."

She'd caught him by surprise and his step faltered for a split second. "No?"

"I'm sorry," she apologized, instantly contrite. "My brother and his wife host the Cinderella Ball. I'm simply observing. I guess I should have explained sooner."

"A shame." He recovered with impressive speed. "Well, I guess a single dance isn't against the rules, right?"

"Not at all."

She glanced over his shoulder toward Chaz. The

blonde and the redhead had disappeared and he now danced with the sultry brunette. She was dressed as Cleopatra, her skirt so tight it was a wonder she could move at all. Perhaps that was why she found it necessary to drape herself over Chaz—so he could drag her around the dance floor without having to do more than shuffle her feet.

"...but if you *were* looking for a husband, what would you want him to be like?"

She forced her attention back to August. What should he be like? Her gaze drifted to Chaz once again. "Intelligent. Straightforward. Protective. Honorable." Her husband had been all those things. At least, when she'd known him.

Sotherland grinned. "So far, so good."

So far, so good? Surely, he didn't think...? No, he didn't, she realized in relief. She could see it in the teasing gleam in his eyes. Cute. She decided to play along. "Oh, but there's more."

He lifted his eyebrows. "Do tell."

"If I were considering a husband, he'd have to be tall, broad-shouldered, have brown hair with whitish streaks, and intense blue eyes. Oh! And a tiny chip in his left canine tooth."

"Darn. Not a chip to be found." He grinned to prove it.

"Oh, dear. I'm afraid that will never do."

He shook his head with a soft click of his tongue. "I guess that means we weren't meant to be."

"I guess not," she responded with a sigh of regret.

"But I notice that fellow behind us has rather intense blue eyes."

A hint of warmth washed across her cheekbones. "Really?"

"Sure enough." He maneuvered them in a tight circle to get a better look. "I admit I'm not the best judge, but he appears on the tall side, too. Not to mention broad-shouldered."

"How...interesting."

"Isn't it?" August murmured. "Too bad his streaks are gray—"

"They are *not* gray!"

"No?" he asked innocently. "My mistake. Now if only we could discover if the poor man has chipped teeth...." Before she could protest, he swerved into the path of the oncoming couple. "Gee, didn't see you folks," he was quick to apologize.

Chaz swung around and looked at them. For a breathless moment, Shayne was certain he'd recognized her. That he, too, felt the hot, sweet emotions that lingered, charging the air between them. But after subjecting her to a swift, impersonal examination, he turned his attention to August. "No damage done."

"Hey. Is that a chipped tooth you have there?"

Chaz's jaw locked and a warning glitter appeared in his eyes. "What if it is?"

"Amazing coincidence, wouldn't you say, my dear?" he asked Shayne. "White streaks, blue eyes, chipped tooth. It's downright magical."

Chaz folded his arms across his chest—a chest that seemed even broader than she remembered. "Buddy, you're startin' to rub me the wrong way. Maybe you should move on before you end up with a few chipped teeth of your own."

"Right you are." He gave Shayne a surreptitious wink, captured Cleopatra in an enthusiastic embrace and half-dragged, half-danced her across the floor.

A silent moment passed while Shayne scrambled for

something to say. Chaz's eyes behind his mask were every bit as piercing as she recalled and having them fixed so steadily on her didn't help her conversational skills. "Mind telling me what that was all about?" he finally asked.

"August was just trying to be helpful."

"Helpful."

"Yes. He…he asked me to describe the man I'd want to marry and…" She shrugged, confessing with painful honesty, "I described you."

"Why?"

"You remind me of someone I once knew." Knew, and considered to be the perfect man. Had August sensed her feelings and decided to do a bit of match-making? Gratitude vied with nervousness. "When my friend saw you and made the connection, he took matters into his own hands."

Chaz's eyes narrowed. "Were you trying to blow him off? Is that why you described me?"

She sensed a harshness in him that hadn't been there before, a molten core tamped under tight control. What would happen if that control ever slipped? She didn't think she'd like to be around as a witness. "I wasn't lying to him, if that's what you're asking."

"Why describe me? It can't just be my resemblance to this other man."

The molten core had splashed closer to the surface and Shayne realized she'd have to respond very, very carefully. "I thought we might be compatible." They had been, once upon a time.

"What about me made you think that?"

Everything. Their past. The way he'd made love to her. The fact that he stood before her after all these years. "It's just a feeling."

The chill coming off him froze her out completely. "I don't trust feelings."

That alarmed her more than anything else he could have said. Had he changed so much? "What do you trust?"

"Not much. I want to see and touch it to believe in its existence. And even then I have my doubts."

Unbidden tears pricked her eyes. Had she and Rafe done that to him? Were they responsible for the coldness that iced his every word? "Why are you here?" she asked helplessly.

"To find a woman."

For a split second hope raced through her. "What woman?"

"Doesn't much matter so long as we can come to terms."

She turned abruptly, the air escaping her lungs in a desperate rush. It hurt to inhale, hurt to blink, hurt to think. "What are your terms?" she asked thinly.

"Lady, we're standing in the middle of a dance floor. Do you really want to negotiate a marriage contract here?"

"We could... We could go downstairs and have a cup of coffee." She desperately needed the warmth to counteract this first, brief bitter-cold conversation. "Would that do?"

"Sure."

Realization struck and she almost burst into hysterical laughter. Her ex-husband—were they considered ex-husbands when the marriage had been annulled?—wanted to sit down and share a cup of coffee with her while discussing what he needed in a new wife. Did life get any stranger than that?

She glanced over her shoulder to where August had

stranded Cleopatra. She'd already picked up a new
swarm of admirers. "Am I taking you away from
someone?"

His hand settled at the base of her spine, filling the
hollow with surprising heat. "No one important." As
though realizing how callous he sounded, he added,
"We weren't on the same wavelength."

They left the floor and the bells decorating her head-
dress and mask swayed, colliding with soft, excited
jangles. For some reason the melodic sound reassured
her. It announced change and spiritual awakening—
both of which she needed very badly.

Chaz flicked one of the golden strands. "I won't
lose you in the crowd with these."

The words seemed prophetic. "It's easy to become
lost."

"No problem. I'd find you again."

He hadn't last time and hurt made her reckless.
"That's assuming you want to find me."

His careless grin was belied by the dead seriousness
of his gaze. "Oh, I'd want to find you."

As they left the ballroom, Shayne glanced toward
the reception line. Rafe and Ella were no longer there.
What would they do if they discovered her with Chaz?
Or was that the idea? Had her brother sent tickets to
both of them in the hopes of sparking this meeting?

Once in the dining room, they bypassed the tables
loaded with every conceivable delicacy and found a
discreet table tucked away in the corner of the room.
"I'll get coffee," Chaz said. "Looks like they have
every sort in creation. What's your preference?"

"Plain and black, please."

"A hot-water-and-beans woman, huh? And here I'd
had you pegged as one of those fake coffee lovers."

"You think I look like the cappuccino type?"

He cocked his head to one side as he assessed her. "I'd say a latte or perhaps a mochaccino."

"Doubled or tripled?"

He regarded her in amusement. "Oh, a grande, at the very least."

"Heavens, no! It has to be a tall skinny halfway between a flat white and a cap. No foam." Her brows drew together as she gave it further consideration. "On second thoughts maybe I should go with a lungo or a poophead."

He held up his hands in surrender and a smile pulled the harshness from his face, hinting at the boyishness she'd once known so intimately. "One black coffee, it is."

"The thicker, the better?" she teased.

"I drink the type you have to cut with a knife and fork. But I'll be a nice guy and make yours a bit weaker if that's what you prefer."

"You want a strong cup of coffee? Maybe you should try—" She'd almost suggested the Costa Rican *tacita de café*, but caught herself at the last minute. Bringing Costa Rica into the conversation would be a dead giveaway.

"Try…?"

"Try asking the *barista*," Shayne replied instead. "I'm sure she'll know which will offer the best jolt for the sip."

To her relief, he appeared to accept her comment at face value. Thank goodness! She didn't want Chaz to know who she was. Not yet. Not until she'd had a chance to spend some time with him. She wanted to discover what had happened over the past nine years and see if they could regain what they'd once shared.

It was a ridiculous dream, as foolish as it was reckless. But she couldn't help herself. Just as she'd been instantly attracted to him that infamous night so long ago, she found that attraction every bit as immediate and powerful the second time around.

"Here we are. Two coffees. Both black." He took a seat opposite her. "I don't believe we've introduced ourselves." He offered his hand. "I'm Chaz from Lullabye, Colorado."

He hadn't volunteered his last name. That would simplify matters. "My first name's Marianna." It was the truth. She'd only adopted her middle name, Shayne, when Rafe had rescued her from her hellish existence in Florida.

"Marianna. Pretty. And why are you here?"

"The same reason most of the people are. I'd like to find a husband." One special, long-lost husband. "What about you?" She struggled not to appear too anxious.

"I'm looking for a wife."

"Why?" she couldn't help asking. "Why here?"

He shrugged. "Someone sent me a ticket."

*Rafe!* "So you came? Just because you received a ticket?"

"I had another reason." He toyed with his coffee cup. "I recently bought a ranch."

So the wanderlust had finally left Chaz McIntyre. "And this ranch requires a wife?"

"Yes." Bald. Abrupt. He spoke the word in a tone that warned he wouldn't take kindly to questions.

Too bad. She had questions and a lot of them. Did he really expect to show up at the ball and entice someone to the altar with just his good looks? He'd be satisfied married to such a shallow, undemanding woman? "Why do you want a wife, Chaz?"

He took a long drink of coffee, as though debating how much to say. She suspected it would be as little as he could get away with. "The ranch is in need of repair. I can handle the structural changes, but not the rest."

"What rest?"

His mouth compressed. "It's a bachelor residence. There isn't a female within miles. The place needs a woman's touch."

She stared at him in disbelief. "You're getting married so you'll have someone to coordinate throw pillows?"

He slammed his mug to the table. "No! I need someone who can create a ho—" With a muttered oath, he looked away, tension vibrating along every line of his body.

"A home?" she finished in a gentle voice.

"Yeah."

He hadn't meant to admit so much. Dusky color rode his angled cheekbones and his features had compressed into taut lines, etched there by more than the sum total of thirty-one years. No doubt they'd been a hard thirty-one years, filled with disillusionment and pain, his face weather-beaten into the sort of creases women found irresistible on men and dreaded seeing in their own mirrors. He thrust a hand through his hair, combing the sun-kissed streaks on top into the crisp nut-brown strands beneath.

"I gather you prefer more than a housekeeper or interior decorator?"

"A lot more."

"And what are you willing to give in return?"

He didn't like the question. "What do you want?" he asked warily.

"That isn't what I asked. I assume you're offering a home and basic creature comforts."

"I'm not a rich man," he warned.

She regarded him steadily. "Then it's a good thing I don't need riches, isn't it?"

He returned her look. No doubt his years of wrangling had helped him sum people up with swift accuracy. "Lay it out for me, Marianna. You're after something. What is it?"

She thought about it, sitting so quietly even the bells on her mask fell silent. He wanted a wife to create a home for him. He'd offered to provide physically for that wife. But what about her emotional needs? What about his? "Will we share a bed?"

"Yes."

"Tonight?"

He answered without hesitation. "Yes."

"And you expect a woman to hop into bed with you after such a short acquaintance?" she asked curiously.

"We'll be married."

"So you gift her with your worldly possessions and she gifts you with her body and a home. That's your idea of a marriage?"

"If you're looking for more than that, you're sitting at the wrong table."

"No love? No affection?"

"I'll treat you well. I'll never hurt you, at least not intentionally."

He was lying. She sensed it with every instinct she possessed. He was a man in desperate need of love, though he'd undoubtedly deny it, just as he'd undoubtedly fight long and hard to hold it at bay. So the real question was... Did she have it within her to give him that sort of unconditional love? It was an even greater risk than the one she'd taken nine years ago. Then, he'd been open and carefree, all too willing to surrender his heart, to give every bit of himself to a woman. She couldn't be certain that man still existed, that once he uncovered her identity, he'd ever come to trust her enough to allow love into his life again.

"Are you interested?"

He asked the question as though her response were of no particular interest. But his hands were clenched around his coffee mug and his eyes were carefully blank. That, more than anything, gave her hope. He was a man determined to keep love out of his life, and yet he'd come to the Cinderella Ball to find a bride capable of creating a home for him.

"Yes, I'll marry you."

Coffee sloshed over the rim of the cup. "I don't recall askin'."

"Now who's playing games?" She didn't give him time to respond. "Do you want to marry me or not?"

He paused for an infinite second. "Okay, fine. But you have to do something for me, first."

"What's that?"

He leaned across the table toward her, his eyes an incandescent blue, full of fierce determination and tightly controlled passion. "Take off your mask."

# CHAPTER TWO

*To my Long-Lost Bride,*

*I'm counting the days until I see you again. It's been almost a year and I can't get you out of my head—or my heart. Your brother sent the annulment papers, but I don't care what they say. You'll always be my wife, the woman who will bear my children, my Forever Love, the person I'll adore until the day I die. You are my sweetness in an often bitter world.*

*I've been working hard these long, lonely months, saving every penny. I know one of your brother's concerns was that I couldn't support a wife. But I've been smart. I invested my earnings and am planning the perfect home for you. It won't be much to start, but it'll be all ours.*

*The Anniversary Ball is just a week away. It's to celebrate the first anniversary of those who married at the Cinderella Ball, and even though our marriage was annulled, I know you'll be there and that this time when we become man and wife, no one can part us. Keep fighting, Shayne. And come back to me.*

*Until I hold you in my arms again...*

TO CHAZ'S private amusement, the bells on Marianna's mask clattered together in discordant protest. "Take off—"

"Your mask. Yes." He lifted an eyebrow. "Problem?"

"I'd rather not," she admitted.

Something about such devastating honesty had him regarding her with acute suspicion. "And why's that?"

"What does it matter what I look like?" It was her turn to clench the coffee mug with white-knuckled desperation. "I don't recall your mentioning that as part of your requirements. You wanted someone who'd turn your house into a home, who'd be willing to live with you in Colorado, who'd—"

"Sleep with me."

It was a wonder the cup didn't shatter in her hands. Did she find the idea of being intimate with him so overwhelming? He'd soon ease her past that particular concern.

"Yes," she acknowledged. "And to sleep with you."

He stood and approached her side of the table. "Don't you think we should have a peek under the masks to make sure we can face each other over the breakfast table every morning?" he asked.

She held him with inky dark eyes, eyes that stirred memories he'd sooner forget. "And if my looks don't appeal, we go our separate ways?"

Dammit! Did she think him so heartless? "I didn't say that."

"So it's not whether or not I can make a home for you that's important. It's whether or not I'm attractive enough to have in your bed?"

He stooped beside her, taking her hands in his. "Honey, in case you didn't know... It doesn't much matter what your partner looks like once the lights are out, so long as part A fits pleasurably into slot B.''

He'd insulted her. It hadn't been intentional, he just had an unfortunate knack for brutal frankness. Hell, he wanted a wife. Or rather, he needed one. If he were perfectly honest, he didn't care how plain-faced the woman he married, so long as she could satisfy his requirements.

He'd had beautiful. If he was forced to take a wife, then this time around he wanted practical.

Chaz studied his prospective bride. He could see her intention to walk away as clearly as if she'd spoken it aloud. But something held her back. Something he couldn't quite understand. Still, he saw it in the slight softening of her chin and the gentling of the anger darkening her passionate brown eyes. A smile flirted with her mouth, a smile as feminine and appealing as any he'd ever seen. Warmth pooled in his gut, stirring a reaction he hadn't felt in far too many years.

''If it doesn't matter, then the mask stays,'' she said. ''You decide. Are you willing to marry, sight unseen?''

Aw, hell. He carefully disengaged their fingers. ''You're asking me to take a lot on faith.''

''You're not a man with a lot of faith, are you?''

''Not a scrap.''

''What happened?'' she asked with the sort of kindness he couldn't handle, the sort of kindness he didn't deserve.

''I lost it long ago.''

''Perhaps someday you'll find it again.''

''If that's what you're holding out for, you're going to be sorely disappointed.'' He straightened, towering over her, and thumped his index finger on the linen-covered surface for emphasis. "I'm offering you a house. I'm offering you a warm bed. The closest you'll get to faith is that I'll remain true to our marriage vows for as long as they legally last. And I'll see that you don't want for anything it's within my power to give. Take it or leave it."

"Just don't expect love?"

"Not a chance in hell."

Her mouth drew together as she weighed his statement, gathering into an unconscious half-kiss that proved a gut-tightening temptation. If she hadn't chosen that moment to speak, he'd have leaned down again and sampled those rosy lips to see if they tasted as luscious as they appeared. "Why should I agree to that sort of a marriage?"

"Frankly, I can't think of a single damned reason." He picked up his coffee cup and downed the contents. Studying the dregs, he considered his words. "Look... I came here to find a wife." He set the mug on the table with a finality she couldn't mistake. "I've given you my reasons and I've been honest about what I can offer in return. Brutally honest. If what I'm selling doesn't coincide with what you're buying, tell me now. There's still time to find new partners."

She stood, as well. "I'm not interested in finding someone else."

"You sure?" Chaz regarded her with unflinching deliberation, allowing just a hint of his annoyance to spill into his gaze. She'd pushed him as far as he intended to be pushed. If she didn't back off soon, he'd take a walk and scout the area for an alternate bride. "I'm not in the mood for games."

"Neither am I. In fact, I only have one last question."

"And what's that?"

"How do you feel about children?"

"The first thing I packed were several guarantees to avoid that particular complication." He held up his hand before she could interrupt. "I'm not opposed to them. I'm just trying to be sensible. Let's work out the kinks in our marriage before introducing babies into the mix."

"But you don't rule them out for sometime in the future?"

"No." He studied her with unrelenting intensity. "How do *you* feel about kids?"

"I love them." She smiled. "If you don't want to have any right away, I'll be happy to adopt any of your employees' children until you are."

That won his approval. "Young ones are in scarce supply around the ranch. But I'll see what I can do."

"I'm curious."

His mouth twisted. "Now why don't I find that surprising?"

"I can't imagine," she teased.

"Go on," he said with a sigh. "Spill it. What are you curious about?"

"How do you decide whether I'm capable of turning your house into a home? What qualifications does your wife need?"

"I think this might be a good time to take our discussion someplace more private. There's a small balcony on one side of the garden. It's probably off limits, but I'm willing to risk it, if you are." He held out his hand, palm up—a hand that mirrored its owner, work-roughened and callused into painful hardness. "Would you mind if we go there?"

Shayne stilled. She remembered that balcony all too

well. That's where she'd first met Chaz. He'd appeared in the garden beneath and, spying her, had done a very poor imitation of Romeo, spouting an amusing "cowboy" version of Shakespeare. And then he'd come after her, scoffing at the circular staircase hidden behind the bushes and instead climbing the trellis adjacent to the balcony. One look into laughter-filled blue eyes set above a cocky grin and she'd been lost. He'd vaulted over the wrought-iron railing and captured her heart the same instant he'd captured her lips. They'd talked for hours, planning a dream life that on the stroke of midnight they'd turned into a reality by speaking vows she'd kept to this day.

She inclined her head, ignoring the clamor of protest issued from silver-voiced bells. "The balcony sounds perfect."

He led the way into the garden, finding the steps concealed behind the shrubbery with unerring accuracy. She preceded him without a word, afraid if she spoke, she'd give herself away. Did he even realize that behind the French doors at the top of the stairway he'd find the bedroom she'd used whenever she and Rafe visited the Montagues on business? Of course, the bed and furniture were now draped in dust covers, the room as asleep as she'd been all these years.

"Okay, Marianna. Let's get down to specifics."

She fought not to react to the name. It seemed such a sham coming from his lips. Worse, it brought back memories of her aunt and of Florida, memories she'd rather not have resurrected. "Go ahead."

"I already told you I live on a ranch. It's a fair size which means it takes up a good bit of my time."

"So you won't be around much?"

"It depends on the season and the workload. I'm

just giving you notice there'll be occasions where you'll spend more hours alone than you might like. Can you handle that?"

"It shouldn't be a problem. I have art commissions that I can work on when I'm at a loose end."

"You're an artist?"

"Those days I'm not managing the family farm."

She'd surprised him. "Then you're familiar with the lifestyle?" he asked in relief. "You understand it'll be isolated."

"I understand that going to town is an all-day affair." At least, it had been on Rafe's coffee *finca* in Costa Rica. "Though I doubt our farm is the same as your ranch, I assume many of the chores will be similar. If so, I can handle your accounts, schedule employees, take care of payroll and run a household."

"Anything you can't do?" he asked in amusement.

"Well... There *is* one rather notable failing. But I'll give just about anything a try. Is that good enough?"

He folded his arms across his chest and lifted an eyebrow. "Care to tell me what that failing is?"

She shook her head. "Not really."

Instead of annoying him, he must have found her confession amusing. A broad grin revealed the tiny chip in his tooth, a chip she'd found quite by accident when they'd first kissed. "I'm supposed to marry a masked woman with one serious failing. More and more interesting."

"It'll give us plenty to learn about each other over the course of our marriage."

"So I've found a woman who likes mystery in her relationships." The amusement died. "Okay. Have it your way."

Astonishment held her silent for a split second. "Then you agree?"

"Fair warning. I have a few secrets of my own. If a bit of mystery between a husband and wife doesn't bother you, it doesn't bother me."

A nerve-racking thought struck. "This secret of yours... Is it anything illegal?"

To her astonishment, his mouth tightened. "Nothing I can be jailed for."

"Oh, Chaz," she whispered, moving close enough to touch his arm. "Is your secret really that serious?"

"Serious enough, masked lady."

What in the world had he done? "Do you regret it?"

"No." His answer was swift and unconditional and all the response necessary in order for her to make her decision.

"Then that's all that matters."

"Not quite. I'm willing to take you sight unseen and accept this serious flaw you possess. But there's one important aspect of our relationship we have to explore before we make a final commitment."

"Is that why you brought me here?"

"Yes."

"So we'd have some privacy?"

"Yes."

She refused to be coy. "Privacy to make love."

He didn't back down beneath her direct gaze. "We need to know for sure. It's an important aspect of a marriage."

The sex had to be good, but wasn't to involve emotions. Didn't he see how wrong that was? "And if we're not compatible?"

"We reconsider."

The bells on her mask issued a quick, urgent warning. "I'm nervous, Chaz," she confessed. "Is that so surprising?"

His eyes were black in the darkness of the night, the distant fairy lights strung through the garden not enough to touch them with color. He turned and leaned against the railing, folding his hands along the top and stared out at the starlit night. She saw his gaze drift past the fanciful gardens and outward toward the stark, uncompromising landscape of the desert. The full moon washed down, blessing it with softness. But the night's shadows cut across the silvery light in hard, harsh strokes, giving lie to the pastoral gentleness. It was a fitting match for the man at her side.

"I noticed you when you first arrived," he said after a bit. "You didn't know that, did you?"

Alarm filled her. Had he seen her unmasked? "When I first arrived?"

"A few minutes before you danced with Sotherland. You came down the steps into the ballroom. Your mask hides a lot, but it didn't hide your eagerness, your impatience to join the party."

*To find him,* she almost corrected. "And?"

"Before you could reach your goal, a rather elderly man stopped you."

She remembered. "He'd twisted his ankle and needed help."

"You helped him."

"That impressed you?" she asked in disbelief. "Anyone would have done the same. It's common decency."

"No one had helped him until you arrived." He glanced at her over his shoulder. "He wasn't the only one, either. There was a young girl sitting by herself, practically in tears. You must have talked to her for ten whole minutes.''

"She reminded me of someone I once knew," Shayne admitted.

"You sent her home, didn't you?''

"She didn't belong. She'd only come because she wanted to escape her home life. I suggested some alternate ways she could accomplish that without marrying a perfect stranger.''

"Unlike you?"

The question hit home. "I'm not eighteen, nor am I trying to escape an unhappy home life.''

"What are you trying to escape?"

"Nothing.'' She took a deep breath, struggling to open herself to him. Once upon a time, she'd have shared her innermost thoughts and feelings with ease. But over the years, she'd become more cautious. "I'm not trying to escape anything, Chaz. I'm trying to find something.''

Tension built along his shoulders and tautened his spine. "Find what?"

Respite from the past. A love she'd lost long ago. "My future.''

"And you think that future's with me?''

"I haven't decided, yet,'' she admitted with perfect candor.

"If you're looking for some sort of fairy-tale romance, you're talking to the wrong man. I'm not interested in love. I'm after someone who's interested in a practical relationship, who's willing to help create a home. A woman with a sense of humor and a generous spirit who'll stick by me when life gets tough.'' He turned and faced her. "Are you that woman?''

"Let me get this straight. I can share a life with you, but not love?"

"Not unless you want a world full of hurt."

"And that's supposed to induce me to marry you?"

"No. That's supposed to make you think long and hard. Are you in the market for practical or are you Cinderella waiting for the prince? Fantasy or reality?"

Didn't Chaz realize? *He* was that prince, their hearts and souls joined on a fateful night nine impossibly long years ago. He might regret ever having met her, but what they'd shared had been special. She refused to believe otherwise. Their joining had been a delicious combination of fantasy and reality. Otherwise, the feelings would have faded over time, only brought to mind on rare occasions, to be examined unemotionally with a sigh of regret or a smile of distantly remembered pleasure.

She faced him, feeling impossibly small and fragile beside his indomitable strength. She had to win this battle of wills. There was no other choice. She had to make him believe in dreams again. "Why don't you kiss me, Chaz, and we'll see whether it's fantasy or reality."

Something dark and powerful moved in his gaze. "All right, sweetheart. Have it your way." His words were pragmatic enough, but the tone told her something far different. It warned of a man fully roused, a man who took what he wanted, no quarter given. "Let me prove that it isn't Prince Charming you're kissing, but the real thing."

"Or perhaps it'll be a little of both."

"Don't fool yourself, darlin'." He captured her in his arms, his hands strong and firm on her back. Then they slid to her hips, settling on the gentle swell flaring beneath her narrow waist. "I intend to see to it that you go into this marriage with your eyes wide open."

"They're open."

"Keep them that way."

Reaching up, he ripped off his mask, revealing the features that had haunted her memory all these years. The boyishness had given way to leaner angles, emphasizing his blade-straight nose and cheekbones set at an interesting slant. His mouth was broad, the lips wide enough to be considered sensuous, yet decidedly masculine. And his chin warned of a man set in his way. But his eyes... His eyes held her, drew her in, denying the coldness of his words. Somewhere behind the barriers of pain, buried beneath years of denial, lay a heart capable of a love so deep, so indomitable, she'd do anything to find it again.

As though sensing the direction of her thoughts, he reached for her mask. "Still intent on keeping this on?"

"Please, don't!" She evaded his hand with a quick twist that stirred her bells to life. She had no choice but to hide her face. Any chance of establishing a relationship with him would end the instant he saw who she was.

Chaz reacted without thought. She shouldn't have run. The primeval urge to hunt forced him to give chase. He couldn't explain what ancient cravings drove him—whether it was the mystery of her features, or the fleet grace of her movements, or the generous womanly curves set in a dainty frame. Perhaps it was something far more basic, man scenting a woman's desire. All he knew was he had to have her. Now.

She paused mid-flight, trapped by the railing, and

spun to face him. Her gown belled out around her and he could hear the nervous give and take of her breath. For a long moment, she stared at him. And then her arms dropped to her sides in unconditional surrender. She was his for the taking and they both knew it.

He offered his hand and she pleased him by slipping willingly into his embrace. She was a contradiction that enticed, her pale hair bound into repressive order at the nape of her neck, while her dark eyes warned of an intensely passionate nature.

"Will you let me keep my mask on?" she asked.

"Keep it, if it's important to you. But if I can't see you, at least let me taste you."

Her eyes fluttered closed, eyes that haunted him in unsettling and unexpected ways. "Chaz…"

Her whisper was sheer temptation, a siren's call pitched to beguile even as it pleaded for his seduction. Her breath mingled with his, the honeyed warmth pulling him closer, demanding that he sample the lush flavor. He wanted to take her mouth, hot and fast. Instead, he drove them both insane with slow and thorough.

He drank, deeply, his thirst ravenous. Her mouth was every bit as soft as he'd anticipated, opening to him without hesitation. They began the ageless dance of lips and tongue and teeth, first gentle, then rapacious, teasing, then deadly serious. He wrapped a hand around her neck, feeling her desperate moan vibrate against his palm. The sound licked through him, piercing straight to a non-existent soul. He knew that distinctive feminine whimper. Knew what it meant. Knew what it demanded of him.

"It's coming, my sweet. I have what you need."

He felt for the zipper at the back of her dress and

lowered it. The metallic rent meshed with the urgent babel of bells. Their mouths melded again and again while his fingers slipped along the smooth expanse of her spine to the hollow above her buttocks. He backed her away from the railing, deeper into the shadows of the balcony. Moonlight cut across her mask, highlighting the ivory beads and golden bells, and revealing the liquid darkness of her eyes. Black eyes. Familiar eyes. Eyes that haunted.

"I'm no prince, sweetheart. I'm all man, blood and bone and as tough as they come."

She shook her head, hair loosened from their embrace slipping in a pale curtain about her shoulders. "You're a man who holds honor dear and protects those in his care."

"You couldn't possibly know that."

"I know."

"You're putting your faith in a man who doesn't believe in such things. Blind faith isn't smart, honey. Not with someone like me."

"That kiss erased any doubts I might have had."

His gaze shifted to her mouth. Her lips were kissed into plump ripeness—damp and swollen and ready to be taken again. "Don't kid yourself. That kiss was lust at its best." He cupped her upper arms, nearly groaning aloud when her dress slipped downward, draping over his hands in silent supplication. Ivory-toned skin peeked through her curtain of hair, stirring an urge so dangerously primitive, he shook with it. "At least our marriage won't be lacking in one area."

"It won't lack in any area. Not if you're willing to give it a chance."

He closed his eyes, speaking through gritted teeth. "A wife. A home. Sex. That's all I want."

"It won't be. Not for long."

"You play a dangerous game, lady."

"It's no game."

Her arms lifted free of her dress and encircled his neck. She was like some untamed mythological goddess. Masked, her hair tumbled in an appealing tangle, bared to the waist, her mouth lifted to his in generous invitation... He unleashed his control and allowed her spell to consume him.

She branded him with her delicate touch, igniting him, setting a wildfire that wiped clean all thought. He leaned into her, fell into her, filling his hands with her lush breasts, filling her mouth with fierce, uncontrolled sweeps of his tongue. The scent of her drove him wild, her taste a distant, yet strangely familiar memory that had him acting on pure instinct. He bit her lower lip, tugging on it. And then he found the fine-boned joining of her neck and shoulder, and finally the pebbled tips of her breasts. Her soft cries of pleasure drove him onward, had him lifting the wide skirt of her gown to give her the completion they both so desperately sought.

"Wait." She stayed his hand. "We can't. Someone might see."

"Don't stop me." His breath labored in his chest and he trembled with the strain of speaking when the moment called for sheer physical expression. It had been so long since he'd had a woman, so long since he'd *wanted* a woman that he was almost mindless with need. "I don't think I can stop now."

"You don't have to. But we can't make love here." She fumbled behind her for the doorknob. "This room's been deserted for years. No one will find us."

If he'd been paying attention, he'd have known the

truth, known whom he held in his arms, understood why her kisses were so familiar, why they made him so frantic, why he could anticipate her every craving and she his. But he simply accepted her comment at face value, accepted that she would know the room was empty, that no one had used it for years, and that it lay silently in wait for the joining of two time-lost lovers.

Moonlight led the way inside and then deserted them, forcing him to rely on scent and sound. For some reason it intensified his arousal, drove the imperative to mate. The rustle of her dress pinpointed her location and he came after her, snatching her from the arms of darkness into his embrace. Her dress was a hindrance soon discarded.

"Where?" he demanded.

Somehow she understood his question. "This way."

Three swift steps led him to a sheet-covered bed. He lowered her to the cool cotton, stripping away her nylons and panties. For a brief instant the moon unveiled itself again and he saw her clearly.

She was white on white, her skin a lustrous pearl on a bed of milky innocence. The only color was the hint of gold in the long strands of hair pillowing her head and textured between her thighs. And her eyes. Huge and black and filled with a woman's vulnerability. For some reason her mask only added to that vulnerability, adorning her with shy mystery.

"I won't hurt you," he whispered.

"I know."

"I'm going to make you mine. Now. But I swear on what little honor I possess I'll marry you afterward."

"I know that, too."

Her certainty cut with whiplike brutality, biting deep and leaving a scar he'd carry for years to come. He didn't deserve such faith. *But he wanted it.* He wanted it as urgently as he wanted to sink into her softness. The moonlight dimmed, like the slow giving of day into the dusky embrace of night. Before it slipped away, he intended to be in her arms, to hold her close so she wouldn't be alone in the dark.

His clothes hit the floor with decisive haste. Once finished, he came to her, wrapping her in warmth as the blackness descended, rolling onto his back with her on top of him. Her mouth scoured his chest with kisses of fire and her hair blanketed him, the strands so long they cloaked him all the way to his hips. He shuddered, tortured by a pleasure so intense he thought it just might kill him. If he could have found his voice, he'd have begged for mercy.

Instead, he flipped her onto her back. His kisses were too hard, too demanding. But rather than complaining, she cupped his face and lifted her mouth for more.

"Tell me this isn't your first time," he said, his voice so raw he barely recognized it as his own.

"It's not my first time."

"I don't know if I can— It's been so long that—"

"I want you. Very badly."

The urge to fill her, to take her, to make her his in the most basic way possible clawed at him. But he fought it. From somewhere he found the few remaining shreds of decency. He touched her with exquisite care, instinctively finding the deliciously feminine spots that would give her the most intense pleasure. The sides of her breasts, the burgeoning tips, the sensitive skin at the lowest point on her belly, the backs of her knees, the upper slope of her buttocks and the creamy softness of her inner thighs. He found them all, anointed each and every one until her body wept for his possession.

And when he'd finished, he took her, filled her, rode the wildness that exploded between them. Only once before had he ever felt such divinity in an act, known such completeness in a physical joining. Memories stormed back, memories he was helpless to rein in. They possessed him as surely as he possessed the woman beneath him. The bells from her mask pealed, as though in joyous welcome. Unable to resist, he gathered her up, sent her surging toward ecstasy. And then he followed her into that glittering realm, at one with her. At one with nature. Heart, body and soul in perfect accord.

But it was an accord not meant to be.

From a great distance he heard the door open and harsh light impaled them. "Oh, excuse me," a voice gasped. Ella's voice. And then... "Oh, dear heaven. Chaz? Is that you? And... *Shayne?*"

# CHAPTER THREE

*To my Long-Lost Bride,*

*It's taken a full year before I could sit down
and write this letter to you. I was so sure, so certain you'd be at the Anniversary Ball. I waited for
you. Waited until dawn broke through the night
sky. And then I left.*

*I'm not even sure why I'm writing this. Maybe
it's my way of saying goodbye. Maybe it's because
I never know when to let go. And I confess, I
rarely give up. What did I tell you on the balcony
that night? Fight until you're unconscious or the
other fella gives up. Well, I'm not out, yet. And I
won't have won this particular fight until you're
in my arms again.*

*I sold the property I'd bought for us and I'm
back wrangling. The ironic thing is…I made a ton
of money off the sale. Even your brother would be
impressed. Ah, hell. What does it matter? There's
only one thing I care about.*

*Dammit, wife. Why weren't you there? Where
have you gone and how do I find you again? Or
was what we shared pure fantasy? Maybe it was
just a dream, a foolish fairy tale. And perhaps I'm
the biggest fool of all for still believing.*

*Shayne… Sweetheart. My Forever Love. Where
are you?*

CHAZ jerked as though he'd been sucker-punched. *"Shayne!"*

"I can explain," she began as Ella made a hasty retreat.

He grabbed the mask and yanked it from her head, flinging it across the room. The elaborate confection caught the moonlight as it soared through the air, glittering with soft radiance while the bells clattered in nervous panic. It hit the floor with discordant finality, sliding into a tangle of painful silence.

Light from the hallway had revealed a lamp on a bedside table, and he fumbled for the switch. Seventy-five watts of incandescent power stabbed through the room with punishing swiftness, darting into every corner and across every object—including her. Never before had she felt so naked. Without her mask, she lay in the middle of the bed still flushed and replete from Chaz's lovemaking...her every thought and expression totally exposed to his unforgiving gaze. She snatched at the bedcover to hide herself. Fortunately, his attention remained fixed on her face, overlooking another of her secrets, a secret that would have been revealed if he'd paid closer attention.

The unnatural calm stretched into an unbearable minute, the tension as punishing as the light. Then he swore, the words harsh and crude, stealing the lingering traces of sweetness from the room.

"It was a trick!" He erupted from the bed. "From the beginning you and your brother have made fools of me."

"No, Chaz. Please. Let me explain."

"What's to explain?" He prowled the room, his nudity making his rage all the more unnerving. "Big brother ripped us apart nine years ago. And now, for some damn reason he's decided to thrust us together again. The master puppeteer yanking the strings."

"That was my fault. You were the only man I ever loved and—"

He approached the bed, magnificent in his rage. "And so now I'm good enough for him? Now that I have property and a home and money, I'm an acceptable husband for his sister?"

"He didn't know you had those things. *I* didn't know."

"He had me investigated, Shayne. There's no other explanation." He snatched his trousers from the floor and thrust his legs into them. "That explains both the ticket and your presence. Well, thanks, but no thanks. I had my strings chopped off by the Beaumonts before. I won't allow it to happen again."

So history would repeat itself. Once more she'd share a single night with the man who'd captured her heart all those years ago. And once more, she'd lose love. No. *No!* She'd been passive for too long, afraid for more years than she could count. And what had it gotten her? She swept from the bed, wrapping the cover around herself like a sarong. Her hair tumbled in a wild tangle about her shoulders, but she didn't care. She faced him down, anger and determination burning within.

"You're not leaving without me."

"That's where you're wrong, Shayne."

"You promised."

"Only because I didn't know who you were."

She had to convince him, no matter what it took. It was their only chance at happiness—a chance he needed as desperately as she, whether he realized it yet, or not. "You came for a wife. Or had you forgotten that minor detail? There's not enough time to find someone else.''

''There's time.'' He thrust his arms into his dress shirt, shoving the tails into his trousers. It hung open, revealing the bronzed chest she'd taken such delight in kissing less than an hour ago. A shudder ran through her at the memory. ''There may not be a lot of choice, but it's not morning, yet.''

''You're going to walk away from what we just shared?''

''As much as I appreciate your generous sacrifice—''

*''Don't!''* The pain was so intense she swayed with it. ''Don't tarnish what happened in that bed. Leave if you want. But don't destroy something so miraculous on your way out.''

For an instant his expression softened and she caught a glimpse of the Chaz she'd once known, the man who'd made her his with a fierce adoration that she'd never forgotten. Would never forget. ''Shayne…'' Her name whispered through the air, ripe with memory.

Behind them the door thrust open. In one instinctive move, Chaz pivoted, planting himself squarely between her and the perceived threat.

''Shayne?'' Rafe called out. ''Are you all right?''

She drew a ragged breath, overwhelmed by what Chaz had revealed. Whether he wanted to admit it or not, he still had feelings for her. No doubt they were buried deep. And no doubt he'd weed them free, if he could. But they were there, nonetheless. ''I'm fine, Rafe. Chaz and I were just getting—'' If it weren't so tragic, she'd laugh. ''We were getting reacquainted.''

''Ella was…concerned.''

"This is between your sister and me, Beaumont," Chaz snarled. "Or were you planning on interfering again?"

"I wanted to make sure she was unharmed."

"She's a big girl now. A few bumps and bruises aren't going to kill her."

Fury glittered in Rafe's eyes and he took a step into the room. "If you mark her in any way—"

This time Shayne took a protective stance in front of Chaz. "It's an expression, Rafe. He didn't mean it literally. Chaz would never hurt me."

"You're pretty confident," he murmured in her ear. "Considering I was on my way out of here when big brother arrived."

Rafe inclined his head, "I'll arrange to have a wedding salon made available." The tiniest of accents had drifted into his voice, warning that he wasn't feeling as equitable as he let on. "Do you have a preference as to the ceremony?"

"Yeah." Chaz bent down and snagged his cummerbund from the floor. "None. I got what I came for."

Rafe drew in a harsh breath and Shayne knew if she didn't act fast, someone was going to leave the room in a lot more pain than when they entered. She turned into Chaz's arms, catching him by surprise. "We can make it a temporary marriage," she said in a low, desperate voice, praying her brother didn't hear. "Just until we find out whether or not I'm pregnant. That'll give me enough time to give you the home you want."

He looked like she'd sucker-punched him. "What the hell are you talking about?"

"You told me you'd packed plenty of protection against that possibility." Her eyes flashed with temper.

"Perhaps you should have taken a moment to *un*pack before coming here."

"I didn't expect to take my bride before taking a wife!"

For some reason that struck Shayne as funny and she couldn't help smiling. "We never seem to get it quite right, do we?"

"Pregnant," Chaz repeated, a shade too loudly. "Damn."

"Preg — *Basta!*" Rafe roared. He stabbed his finger at Chaz. "You will finish dressing and present yourself in the library within the next five minutes. I will have a priest standing by."

"And if I refuse?"

"You would allow her to bear your bastard? It is your style, yes?"

Chaz went white, his hands collapsing into fists. Shayne stared from one man to the other in alarm. Something unspoken passed between the two, something she didn't have a hope of understanding. Whatever it was, it locked them in a battle of wills, an explosive edge of violence burning between them, fighting for expression.

Without knowing what had set them off, she had no hope of diffusing the situation. Still, she could try. "Could we calm down and discuss this rationally? What's going on?"

"Nothing that need concern you," Rafe replied. "Your husband-to-be and I are simply reaching an understanding. Do you agree to my terms, Mr. McIntyre? You'll marry her?"

"You'll regret this, Beaumont."

"I don't doubt it." Rafe's mouth pulled to one side and he shrugged. "But she's my sister. I'll do whatever it takes to make her happy. For some strange reason, she thinks you're capable of doing that. Five minutes." Without another word, he turned and left the room.

"Chaz…?"

"Don't. Don't say another word." He searched the room for his boots. Finding them kicked beneath a drape of sheet, he sat on the edge of the bed and pulled them on. "You heard your brother. You'll have your heart's desire in five short minutes. Do you plan to dress for your wedding or is that bedcover your gown of choice?"

"I didn't intend to deceive you, Chaz, any more than I intended to end up—" She gestured toward the bed. "I just wanted to have time to get to know you again before you found out who I was."

"Honey, I recognize a setup when I see one. A willing woman, a convenient bed, a relative at the door. It's as old as the hills."

"But—"

"Enough, Shayne." He shot her a look that silenced her more effectively than anything else could have, one that combined a bitter cynicism with an underlying fury. "You have precisely thirty seconds to put on some clothes, or I swear I'll drag you downstairs the way you are."

She didn't waste any more energy talking. In one swift move, she dropped the bedsheet while sliding her gown over her head. Underpants and heels followed. She didn't bother trying to wiggle into her stockings. Beneath her floor-length skirt, it was doubtful anyone would notice. Except for her hair, she'd pass muster. Chin held high, she started for the door.

Chaz stepped forward to block her path. An odd

expression slipped into his gaze, an expression she'd known long ago, one that was protective and caring and almost loving. Tears of longing pricked her eyes. "Shayne." Even her name came on winds from the past. "We can't go back."

"I know." She returned his look, regret and hope mingling as one. "But we have the future. We can chose which path we take from here."

A tender smile touched his mouth even as he shook his head. "That path was decided a long time ago. I'm not the man you knew. What you're doing will only cause a world of hurt."

"Only if you choose to hurt me."

The tenderness seeped away, leaving behind desolation. "I can't do anything else. It's not too late, Shayne. Tell your brother you've changed your mind."

"I haven't changed my mind, Chaz. Not in nine years. Not in ninety."

"What you feel is a dream. It isn't real."

"Then I hope I sleep forever." The truth was, she'd *been* sleeping. She'd slept for the past nine years. But she was awake now, brought to life by a single kiss. She couldn't go back to that other existence, even if she wanted to. Life awaited her, a life with Chaz.

His mouth settled along grim lines. "So be it. Let's hope your dream doesn't turn into a nightmare."

Thrusting open the door, he gestured for her to precede him. And as she passed she had the crazy impression that he feathered a kiss on top of her head. Of course, she was mistaken. He was furious with her. Furious at her deception, at Rafe's insistence that they marry, at being caught in the machinations of the Beaumonts once again. Any feelings he might have

for her, she'd destroyed when she'd opened her heart,
while cautiously masking her face.

*Her mask!* Spinning around, she darted past him and
back into the room. She didn't know why it felt so
urgent to recover the mask, but it did. The bells chattered an urgent greeting as she looped the elastic band
over her arm.

"What are you doing, Shayne? You don't need that
any longer."

"I know. I just wanted to have it."

He lifted an eyebrow. "A souvenir?"

"Is that so difficult to believe?"

"I thought souvenirs were to mark occasions you
want to remember. Not those you'd rather forget."

"And you'd rather forget tonight?" she demanded
in a rare display of anger.

"There's only one thing about this evening I care
to remember." He lifted the mask dangling from her
arm and plucked free a strand of bells. "The rest will
haunt my memory without any reminders. Now do we
join your brother, or do we put an end to this farce?"

"We join my brother." She touched his arm as he
drew level with her, feeling the heavy cording of
work-hardened muscle beneath her hand. Tension ra-
diated from him. Did her mere touch do that? If so,
there was hope for them yet. "You had a reason for
marrying, Chaz. That hasn't changed. I promise I'll do
whatever I can to help you achieve your goal. But I
was serious earlier. If I'm not pregnant, I'll leave if
that's what you want. All I'm asking is that you give
us a chance."

As close as they stood, she could see the implacable
set of his jawline, the tight swallow that moved the
bronzed column of his throat. A flare of emotion

sparked in his eyes, before being swiftly doused. "It won't work, sweetheart," he said ever so gently. "Maybe, long ago. But not now."

*"Why?"*

"Because I have nothing left to give. If I ever knew love, it was so long ago I can hardly remember."

A fierce determination seized hold. "Then I'll find it for you. I can. I will!"

"No, Shayne. You won't."

She could scarcely contain her frustration. "I don't understand. Why won't you let me help you? We could find what we once had. I know we could."

His gaze fastened on hers, the expression cold and clear and absolute. "Because I don't want this thing you call love. Not from you. Not from anyone. It's all a lie. And I swear. If you wrap up those lies in pretty declarations of undying love, I'll send you back to your brother before the words even hit the air. Are we clear about that?"

As clear as the sound of her heart breaking. She shivered and the bells pealed a mournful dirge in response. "Yes, Chaz. We're clear."

Chaz stood in front of the priest, deaf to the words being spoken. Only one thought filled his head: he shouldn't have told Shayne the truth. He could have made his objections clear without being so harsh. Maybe then he wouldn't have seen the desolation that filled those huge, dark eyes of hers. Or felt the physical blow her pained gasp had caused. Or heard the jarring clash of bells as she'd jerked free of him, walking away with a fragile dignity that nearly unmanned him.

He slipped his hand into his pocket and fingered the

strand he'd stripped from her mask. Honesty was best, under the circumstances. That way she'd know right from the start what to expect from their marriage.

Chaz suddenly realized there'd been an interminably long silence. While he'd been lost in thought, something significant had happened. Something that had caused everyone in the room to turn and glare at him. "Er... I do?" he said hopefully.

"Oh, Chaz," Shayne whispered, tears filling her lush brown eyes, eyes he could lose his soul in.

He sighed. "Dammit, Shayne. What have I done now?"

Rafe slammed his fist against Chaz's bicep. "*Bárbaro!* She said no to you."

"She said...? Excuse us for a minute." He grasped Shayne's elbow and hustled her off to one side of the room. "What's going on?"

She bowed her head. "I can't go through with this. I can't allow Rafe to force you to marry me. *I* won't force you to marry me."

"You don't understand."

"Yes, I do." She spared a quick glance at her watch. "There's still time. I can help you find someone else. Someone who could—"

"Not a chance," he interrupted. "We're doing this here and now."

"But you said—"

"You were right earlier. You could be pregnant."

She had trouble meeting his eyes, a blush blooming across her cheeks. "If I am, we can deal with it then."

"We'll deal with it now." He released his breath in a rough sigh and bent his head closer to hers. Her scent threatened to drive him crazy, but he rather no one overhear their conversation. It wouldn't be fair to

Shayne. "Listen to me, sweetheart. Once I realized the consequences of what we'd done, I'd have forced you in front of a priest, whether you and your brother agreed or not."

"No!" she instantly denied. "When you found out it was me, you were going to leave."

"Yeah, I was. I admit it. If your brother hadn't stopped me, I'd have taken off. But not to find another bride. You have to believe me, Shayne. I'd have come back for you. It was only the shock of discovering who you were and having to deal with your brother again that caused me to react the way I did."

"You don't want to marry me, Chaz. I know you don't."

He leveled her with a single hard look. "Honey, I don't want to marry anyone. I didn't have any choice before I got here and I sure as hell don't have any choice now. Neither do you. The minute you tumbled into that bed with me, you sealed your fate."

He'd said too much. Curiosity dawned in her gaze. "What do you mean you didn't have any choice before you came?"

"I warned you that I had a few secrets of my own."

"This secret... Rafe knows, doesn't he? That's what you two were talking about."

"I'm guessing he does. Not that that changes anything." He jerked his head toward the cluster of people waiting for them. "Time to finish what we started."

"And if I say no again?"

"You won't. You're bent on redeeming me, remember?"

"I thought you were beyond redemption."

"I am." He offered a crooked smile. "But you're

a woman. So you'll try, anyway." He'd insulted her again. Unfortunately, he suspected it wouldn't be the last time.

"Once we know for certain I'm not pregnant, I'll end the marriage," she assured.

Her promise should have relieved him. Perversely, he found himself thoroughly annoyed. "You'll stay until you've fulfilled your promise to make a home for me. *Then* you can go if that's what you want." Maybe.

"It will be."

"Fine. Now get back over there and tell them you've changed your mind. It's a long drive to Colorado. I'll want to leave for the ranch as soon as you're packed."

This time when they resumed their positions in front of the priest, he paid attention. Several minutes into the ceremony, another painful nudge from Rafe's fist prompted him to repeat his own vows. Not that he needed any prompting. He hadn't been lying to Shayne. Once he'd realized the potential results of their rather enthusiastic reunion, he'd have been back on her doorstep demanding marriage.

Gathering her hands in his, he spoke the required words. If anyone noted that he omitted the word "love" they didn't call him on it. But he knew Shayne felt the impact and silently cursed again. Why did she leave herself open to such hurt? She was a fool to marry him. And he was an even bigger fool to let her. In her heart, she was still that naive seventeen-year-old, believing in miracles and fairy tales.

Well, life with him would soon disabuse her of that notion.

"You have rings you wish to exchange?" the priest asked.

"Sorry, I don't—"

"Allow me," Rafe interrupted, slipping his hand into his pocket.

Chaz forced himself not to move, not to knock loose a few perfect white teeth set in an arrogant mouth. Any doubts that he'd been set up vanished. "All the details planned, right down to the rings, is that it, Beaumont?"

"I like to be prepared."

Chaz swiveled, lowering his voice so only the two of them could hear. "Then start preparin', *brother*. Next time we meet you and I are going to exchange more than words. And one of us is crawlin' away from the meeting wishing he'd never played God with my life."

"If that will make you feel better, you may try to —er—make me crawl. So long as you treat my sister well, what you do to me is immaterial." Rafe forced the ring box into Chaz's hand. "But if you hurt her, I will make your life a living misery."

"Too late, Beaumont. You did that already."

Beside him, Shayne caught his arm. "Chaz? Is everything all right?"

He bit back the words he longed to vent. Words that would make a mockery of the vows they'd just uttered. "Everything's fine."

Thumbing open the jewelry box, he silently swore. Beaumont had taken tickets from the Cinderella Ball and fashioned them into wedding bands. Of course, they fit perfectly.

The minute their union had been blessed, Chaz gathered his wife into his arms. She lifted her gaze to meet his and he saw there an inner strength that had been barely perceptible nine years ago. Time and experience had forged that strength with steel. He wasn't the only one who'd walked the painful side of life and fought back. And yet she still retained the full depth of a woman's heart, open to the possibility of love, no matter how remote.

"I'm sorry," he murmured beneath his breath.

"Sorry that you married me?"

"No. Sorry that our marriage will hurt you."

Leaning down, he captured her mouth, drinking in the taste of her along with the knowledge that she'd soon live with him as his wife. That for a few short weeks he'd have the fulfillment of a dream—a painful irony now that he no longer believed in dreams. But for some reason, he found his cynicism fading, found that all he could think about was the woman in his arms and the sweetness of her kiss. She opened to him, giving what he refused to take by force, offering all of herself despite the threat he posed.

Ever so gently, he released her. "You need to pack. We'll leave as soon as you're ready."

"I'll help," Ella offered.

Rafe stepped forward and embraced his sister. "Your husband and I will wait for you in my office."

She returned his hug with unmistakable enthusiasm and Chaz nearly groaned aloud. It annoyed him no end to see her bestowing her affections on such undeserving recipients. First him. Now Beaumont. Did the woman have no sense of self-preservation?

"No fighting," Shayne warned in a whisper that carried to all corners of the room.

"We'll behave." Rafe shot Chaz a pointed look. "At least we'll try."

Chaz shook his head. "One of us will try."

The other would beat the living hell out of an arrogant coffee farmer at the first wrong word. He cheered up as they left the room. With any luck at all, that word would come within minutes of them gaining some privacy. He worked hard on stoking his temper as they traversed the maze of corridors to Beaumont's office.

"It's fascinating, the information one can acquire," Rafe announced the moment they'd entered his office. "Wouldn't you agree?"

Chaz flexed his fist. That sounded remarkably like a wrong word to him. "Such as my ring size?"

"Ring size, hat size, boot size." Rafe indicated a thick folder centered on his desk as he moved out of reach. "It is all documented. Would you care to see the file?"

Somehow, it seemed undignified to chase the man across the room in order to sock him. Chaz decided to hang tight a bit longer. The instant Beaumont came close again, he'd pop him one. In the meantime... "You had me investigated." It wasn't a question. "That's pretty damn personal information you've got there. If I didn't know better, I'd swear your PI slithered into bed with me."

Rafe regarded Chaz without amusement, his silvery eyes like splinters of ice. "Perhaps she did. I didn't inquire as to her methods. I merely paid well for the results she provided." He crossed to the liquor cabinet. "A drink before you go?"

Chaz bared his teeth. Yeah, sure. Bring it on over. He might even take half a second to drink it down before knocking Beaumont's teeth out. "Whiskey. And for the record, I didn't sleep with your investigator." Now why the hell had he said that? He didn't owe the man an explanation. If anything, Beaumont owed *him*. And he'd be only too happy to collect.

For the first time, Rafe's expression eased. "I know. I also know precisely how many women you've been with since my sister. That information is the only reason you are now married to Shayne, my friend."

Fury seized hold, satisfyingly hot and just begging for expression. "You had no right!"

To his intense annoyance, Rafe inclined his head in complete agreement before crossing to hide behind his desk. The coward! He set the two glasses on the mahogany surface and nudged one in Chaz's direction. "So Ella has told me and on more than one occasion."

Aw, hell. Now why did he have to go and be friendly? "Glad we got that straight," Chaz growled. "Can't go nosing around in a man's private business."

"I would feel precisely the same if our positions were reversed," Rafe commented with disgusting affability. He opened the humidor on his desk and finding it empty, released his breath in a disappointed sigh. "It is just as well," he said, snapping it closed. "My wife doesn't approve and I would pay the consequences if she were to catch me."

Chaz grinned, despite himself. "It's one vice I've managed to avoid. Probably the only one."

"Quite self-destructive," Rafe conceded. "Ella calls it a nervous habit, a crutch. Ridiculous, of course. Still... I have the urge to indulge, particularly in moments of stress. So perhaps she is right, after all."

"I gather this is a moment of stress."

"Hell, yes. Don't you think so?"

They shared an instant of perfect accord, an accord bound to be destroyed the moment one of them chose to speak again. Chaz waded on in, only too happy to have them back on more familiar footing. "It didn't have to be that way. If you'd just butted out—"

"You don't know the whole story, McIntyre. You don't know the life Shayne has lived or you'd understand why I protect her so fiercely."

"That's no longer your concern."

"That's where you are wrong, my friend. Shayne will always be my concern. But I am willing to give her into your keeping. For now."

"Dammit, Beaumont. She's a woman, not property. She's not yours to give any more than she's mine to take."

"But she is yours to protect." The warning glitter had returned to silver-gray eyes. "See that you do so."

"More threats?"

"Yes."

At least he didn't bother with false denials. "I wouldn't let anything hurt her."

"I believe you." There was no doubting Rafe's sincerity. "But I am more concerned about *your* hurting her than any outside force."

Chaz tossed back his whiskey and slammed the glass to the table. "I *won't* hurt her," he lied desperately.

"Not on purpose, perhaps. Still... You have become a hard man, a ruthless man. Hard, ruthless men can crush tender young things beneath their boot heels without even realizing it."

"Not Shayne."

"Let us hope not." Rafe fingered the folder on his desk. "There's one other subject I wish to address before she joins us."

Dammit all! "What now?"

"Relax, McIntyre. It's simply an offer."

"Fine. Say what you need to and let's end this farce."

"My investigator has turned up quite a lot of interesting information."

"And?"

Rafe looked at him. "And if you ever need my help, you have only to ask."

Chaz released his breath in a harsh sigh. He could take insult at the suggestion. Hell, it would be easy. He could allow his pride and anger to drive him to offer the sort of physical response he'd been longing to since he'd first set eyes on Rafe Beaumont. Didn't his hands ache to curl into fists and pummel something?

Instead, he stood and leaned across the desk, offering the hand of friendship to his brother-in-law.

"Thanks," he said, and meant it. "I'll do that."

# CHAPTER FOUR

*To My Long-Lost Bride,*

*I dreamed of you last night. Three years have passed, and yet still, I dream of you. Your scent surrounded me, consumed me, made me believe for just one short instant that you lay beside me. I could hear your voice, shy and yet edged with a woman's passion. I could see your eyes, as dark as the night sky, filled first with laughter and then with warmth and finally with a love I've never seen before...or since. Does it sound trite to say your skin was like satin? Your hair a silken waterfall that streamed over us like golden sunshine in a moonlit room?*

*Have you any idea how you linger in my mind? How, until I hold you in my arms again I'll never know peace? Have you any idea how many nights I've awoken, desperate for one last touch, one final word? Desperate for the completion no other woman can provide? You haunt me, my love. You steal my soul and make me long for the impossible. Whenever I look at a woman, all I see are the ways she doesn't compare to you.*

*I love you, sweet wife. My Forever Love. There will never be anyone but you.*

LATE afternoon sunshine slanted across the Colorado landscape and settled on a structure as hard and rough as the man beside her. "*This* is your home?" Shayne asked.

"No," Chaz corrected in a tone curiously void of expression. "This is my house. It's your job to turn it into a home."

Shayne studied the sweeping lines of the huge ranch house with ill-concealed apprehension. Structurally, it needed work. The porch steps sagged and the roof had been patched more than once. The clapboard siding hadn't seen fresh paint in years and the overflowing gutters looked like they provided hearth and home for any number of woodland creatures. The grounds surrounding the house weren't any better. The patch of earth that might have been a garden long ago was unkempt and gasping beneath dead weeds and thatch. But that particular project could wait until spring.

Assuming she was still here come spring.

She touched her belly with a tentative hand. Had Chaz's child taken root from their one explosive encounter? In a few short weeks she'd know. In the meantime, she could only hope. "Tell me what you'd like done."

"Nothing out here. I'll take care of that part. Your skills are needed inside."

Shayne eyed the warped front door. If the inside was as bad as the exterior, she was in deep, deep trouble. She took a steadying breath. She could do this. If she wanted to build a life with Chaz, she would damn well find a way to whip this slapped-together concoction of wood and nails and pasteboard into a home. "Show me."

He led the way, climbing the steps and forcing the door inward with his shoulder. Shayne followed. She hesitated on the threshold, then stepped boldly

across—not held in her husband's arms as a newlywed
might expect, but trailing behind, about as welcome
as a barefoot guest arriving at a black-tie-and-tails dinner party. Any bridelike feelings she might have harbored vanished with that single step.

For the first time she wondered why creating a home
was so important to Chaz. Why did he need a wife,
when an interior decorator would have done just as
well? She struggled to recall what he'd told her. Not
much. And yet, it had seemed so important to him.

Important enough to enter into a marriage he clearly
didn't want.

A short, grizzled cowpoke appeared from the bow-
els of the house. "Boss, we got trouble and more trouble."

Chaz sighed. "Now why doesn't that surprise me?"
He inclined his head in her direction. "Shayne, this is
my foreman, Penny. Penny, my wife."

The foreman ran a hand over his stubbled jaw,
studying her with open curiosity. "Maybe she oughta
take door number one."

"Door number...? Aw, hell. What's behind door
number one, old man? Or should I say...who?"

"The Donna woman's in your office. Gave her that
room since I figured she wouldn't do too much poking
around behind your back. Can't see her riffling
through your desk on the sly, can you?"

"Not really. And behind door number two?"

"Mojo."

This time Chaz's curse was a bit more virulent.
"What's his problem now?"

Penny drew himself up to his full height, which
wasn't much. But what little he possessed was all attitude. "He heard you went and got yourself hitched."

"Heard it from you, no doubt, since you're the only one I told."

"Be that as it may, he got hisself in a real snit over it. If you want I'll get Jumbo to deal with him. Jes' don't ask the boys to go up against the Donna woman. She scares 'em spitless."

"But not you, right?"

"Keep it up, boss man," Penny warned. "Ride me a little harder and I'll hightail it over to the Winston spread. That little Cami girl said I could have a job whenever I wanted."

"Working for their foreman?" Chaz folded his arms across his chest. "Now that I'd like to see. You and Gabby couldn't agree on the color of the sky. Hell, you'd claim a cow was a bull, just to avoid being on the same side of an argument with him."

Shayne stifled a groan. No doubt these two could exchange insults until— Until the cows came home seemed an appropriate expression, given the circumstances. And if it avoided dealing with the individuals waiting for her husband's attention, no doubt they'd still be standing here come Christmas. Time to take charge.

"Chaz, if you'd go talk to Mojo, I'll speak with Donna. Penny, do you think you could bring us some coffee while we wait?"

The man took instant umbrage. "I'm no cook."

"I'm well aware of that. But I doubt there's a foreman alive who doesn't make a better cup of coffee than the resident cook."

Wicked amusement lit the old man's expression. "Best not be sayin' that anywhere around Mojo."

"The Mojo who's in the kitchen in a snit?" she asked fatalistically.

"The one and same."

"And he is...?"

"The resident cook. Mojo, git it? More joe? Not meanin' to point out your ignorance, but joe's coffee, in case you was wondering."

Great. Just great. She hadn't spent two minutes on the premises and already she'd insulted someone. "Would you mind terribly getting the coffee since I doubt Mojo will?"

"Yes, ma'am, I would mind." Heaving a tremendous sigh, he relented. "But seein' as how you're new here and all, I'll fetch some. Jes' this once, though. Hear?"

"Thank you. That's very sweet of you."

Penny scowled. "Do something nice for a body and see how they repay you." He stomped down the hallway. "Insult you, that's what they do. Sweet. Hah!"

"I don't think this is a very good idea," Chaz began.

"You'll join us as soon as you've spoken to Mojo, won't you?"

"Shayne—"

She ran her hand along his arm. She'd been aiming for reassurance and came away with a sweep of desire so strong she trembled with it. How was that possible? The nine years they'd been parted should have lessened those feelings. Instead, she couldn't look at him, couldn't touch him, without wanting to find her way back into his arms...and into his heart.

"You married me to act as your wife. At least, I think that's one of the reasons. Let me do my job, Chaz. I can sit with Donna for a short time and share a cup of coffee without turning it into a disaster."

"Don't count on it," he muttered.

"Either you trust me or you don't."

"It's not a matter of trust." He thrust his hand into his hair, tumbling the nut-and-wheat-colored strands into attractive disorder. "First off, her name isn't Donna. It's Doña Isabella. Doña Isabella Madalena Vega de la Cruz."

Interesting. "And second?"

"And second... Aw, hell, Shayne."

"She's one of your secrets, isn't she?"

Lines of tension bracketed his mouth, confirming her guess. "She's part of one. I just don't want her telling you something that should come from me. You don't deserve that."

He was protecting her! The knowledge ignited a tiny spark of hope, hope that she'd nurture with every bit of determination she possessed. "Then I'll make sure she doesn't tell me. Will that do?"

"I guess it'll have to."

"Where's your office?"

He gestured toward a door off to her left. "Through there. I'll join you as soon as I can."

She smiled. "It'll work out, Chaz."

"Not likely." He cupped the nape of her neck and drew her close. His mouth slipped across hers in a brief kiss. An instant later he returned for another, this one harder, edged with unchecked passion, a plea and a promise and a demand all wrapped up in one. "I have an idea."

For some reason her eyelids refused to lift. "What's that?"

"Why don't we let our unwelcome visitors sit and stew awhile. We can sneak upstairs and catch up on nine years of waiting. With any luck, they'll be gone by the time we return."

Her eyes flickered open at that. "Am I the lesser of two evils?"

"No. You're the escape from two evils." His mouth scalded a path along her jawline, found her ear and unhinged her with the warmth of his breath. "You're an oasis, water in the middle of an endless desert, life in a barren jumble of rock and dust."

She knew this man—he wasn't the Chaz she'd married, but the one she'd fallen in love with once upon a time. She silently rejoiced at his return, relieved beyond measure to discover that he hadn't totally disappeared. With a little effort, perhaps she could coax him from the hard, cold shell in which he'd encased himself. Maybe. If she were very, very careful. "I wish we could go upstairs and hide there forever," she confessed with devastating honesty. "Just the two of us."

"We can." He urged her closer into a sweet tangle of arms and legs. "Put on your mask, wife, and we'll pretend we're two strangers with no past and no future to torment us. Just the pleasure of the moment, for as long as that moment lasts."

Pain returned, swift and sure. "And when it ends?"

"We'll deal with that. But, later. Much later."

"I wish…"

"Wish what?"

She fixed her gaze on him, wondering if he sensed all she found so difficult to express. "I wish last night meant more to you than a quick tumble in bed. I wish today could, too."

She'd said the wrong thing. His expression closed over and he pulled back, a wintry breeze washing away the heat of passion. Any cracks in his shell had been swiftly repaired. The abrupt change brought tears to her eyes, tears she hid beneath a protective sweep of lashes.

"I warned you before we married."

"I know."

"Don't ask for more than I can give."

Her mouth tilted to one side, tender amusement easing the pain. "Sorry to disappoint you. But I'm going to keep asking."

"Then brace yourself, sweetheart. Because I'm gonna keep refusing."

"That's up to you." She gathered what remained of her self-control. "Why don't we take care of business? I suspect it will make our time together all the more special when we do finally indulge."

He snagged the front of her blouse and tugged her close again, branding her with a final kiss. "Count on it. And count on the fact that I intend to indulge at our earliest convenience."

A ferocious hunger had sparked deep in his eyes, like that of a starving animal, stumbling across an unexpected cache of food. Understanding dawned. A starving animal would fall on the food with a voracious appetite that demanded instant gratification, knowing it could be taken from him at any minute. "You think that what we feel for each other is going to vanish, don't you?"

"There's not a doubt in my mind," he confirmed. "One day we'll wake up and all we'll have between us is hot desert and hard rock."

"If that day ever arrives, you won't have to ask me to leave. I'll go of my own accord."

He inclined his head in agreement, but something held her in place. Something that urged her to take him in her arms and swear her undying love. To prom-

ise that the love she felt would survive anything. That
now that they'd found each other, nothing would ever
part them again. But caution rode her every bit as hard
as it did him. She stepped away, finding it more difficult than she thought possible.

"I'll go introduce myself to Doña Isabella."

"I won't be long."

They went in opposite directions, an irony not lost
on Shayne. Opening the door to Chaz's office, she
braced herself to face the Doña and whatever secret
Chaz was protecting. It only took a single glance to
recognize the woman as a formidable presence.

She sat perfectly erect in the chair opposite Chaz's
desk, her spine so rigidly straight, Shayne suspected it
could be used as a measuring stick. She didn't turn,
but kept her attention focused on a point square in the
center of the wall across from her, her hands folded
in her lap, her chin set at a imperious angle. It wasn't
until Shayne came into her line of sight that the
woman cast a black-eyed glance in her direction, her
magnificent gaze filled with a rebellious life at direct
odds with her inflexible frame. How curious.

"Doña Isabella, I'm Shayne McIntyre. Chaz's wife.
I apologize for keeping you. We've only just arrived."

"Wife?" That captured the woman's full attention
and a hint of emotion moved across sharply proud
features. "So he has done as I requested. I confess I'm
surprised."

Instead of taking the chair behind Chaz's desk,
Shayne chose the adjoining one. It was a small gesture,
but one she hoped the Doña would take as a concil-
iatory sign. "Why does our marriage surprise you?"

Her ravenlike eyes fastened on Shayne, quick and
clever and glistening with a shrewd intelligence. "I

did not think he would find a woman willing to join with him.''

"I was more than willing.''

Her hooked nose was perfectly shaped to emphasize her sniff of disdain. "That does not endear you to me.''

Shayne regarded her in amusement. "Do I need to endear myself to you?''

"If you wish my cooperation, you will do everything within your powers to make me happy.''

Curiouser and curiouser. "I've ordered coffee. Would that be a good start?''

"No. I drink tea.''

"A shame," Shayne said calmly, seeing through the woman's game and playing along. "I suspect Penny would consider it an offense to the cowboy way of life if I were to ask him to fix you some.''

A spark of laughter flickered briefly before dying an icy death. "He is a rude old man.''

"I quite like him. He struck me as someone who offers an honest opinion.''

"Offers it freely and often. Hardly an appropriate attitude for an employee.''

Shayne lifted an eyebrow. "Do you want me to speak to him about his attitude?''

"Would it do any good?''

"None.''

"Then what would be the point?''

Shayne leaned closer, lowering her voice. "Sheer wicked enjoyment.''

Doña Isabella released a snort of laughter just as the door opened behind them. Penny entered, carrying two steaming mugs of coffee. "The coffee's black. Don't believe in ruining a good cup o' joe with anything but whiskey." He thumped the heavy porcelain mugs onto the desk between the two, eyeing the women suspiciously. His grizzled brows drew together. "What? Whatcha lookin' at me that way fer?"

The two women shared a moment of pure feminine understanding. "Thank you for the coffee, Penny," Shayne said as demurely as she could manage. "I hope it wasn't too much trouble."

"Yeah, it was. Not that you two give a hot da—" One glance from the Doña had him backpedaling toward the door. "Dang. A hot dang. If the boss wants me, I'll be out in the barn where the critters don't look at ya funny."

The instant the door had slammed behind the foreman, Doña Isabella gave a sharp nod. "I've reached a decision," she announced. "I've decided that you'll do."

Shayne's brows drew together. "Thank you, seems the appropriate response. Though I'm not quite sure why."

"McIntyre hasn't told you about me, has he?"

"Not yet."

She gave another snort of displeasure, which impressed the heck out of Shayne since the Doña somehow managed to retain her regal air while making the sort of noise capable of cracking glass. It was quite a feat. "Then I'll wait until he does before rendering my verdict."

"And you'll wait because…?"

"Because I want to be certain that you'll remain his wife once you know why I'm here."

"I see," Shayne murmured.

It was a lie and they both knew it, but apparently the Doña intended to let it pass. Clearly this had to do

with the secret Chaz had mentioned on the balcony
the night they'd made love. When she'd asked him if
it was anything illegal, he'd replied, "Nothing I can
be jailed for." Somehow it involved this woman.
But...*how*?

"...and do what I pay you to!" Chaz's voice roared
through the thick oak door. A loud thwack punctuated
his shout. "Is that the best you can do? Hell, you can't
even throw straight, you ham-fisted excuse for a
cook!"

Shayne started in alarm. Now what? "Excuse me,
please."

Hurrying to the door, she yanked it open. Chaz
stood with his back to her, shaking his fist at a huge,
muscle-bound giant of a man who was rapidly disappearing down the hallway. From the way her husband's muscles were knotted beneath his shirt, he'd
soon give physical expression to his anger. She hastened to close the door. It didn't take any great mental
acuity to realize Chaz and the Doña were at odds. No
point in giving her more ammunition to use against
her husband. Now she just had to figure out why he
was also at odds with Mojo.

"What's going on?" she whispered.

"Just explaining the facts of life to my mule-headed
idiot of a cook." He raised his voice. "My mule-
headed, idiot, soon-to-be-unemployed cook."

"I don't understand. Why is he so upset over our
marriage?"

Chaz glanced at her over his shoulder, his expression reflecting a wariness that cut to the quick. At a
guess, he didn't know how she'd respond to the situation and if there'd been time, she'd have blistered
him for it. "I guess I should have spoken to him be-

fore I left and warned that I might be bringing home a wife. But since I didn't know for sure I was going to find someone, I—''

"Chickened out?" she interrupted without giving due thought to the ramifications of her comment. "Considering the size of him, I don't blame you."

Chaz's eyes narrowed, irritation vying with amusement. To her relief, his sense of humor got the better of him. "You think that's intimidating, you oughta see him with a meat cleaver in his hand." He nodded to the front door off to her right.

Shayne's breath stopped in her throat. A meat cleaver was imbedded deep in the wood. Her knees wobbled. "He..." She gulped. "He *threw* that at you?"

"Aw, hell, honey. He wasn't serious or I wouldn't be standing here. He was just punctuating some of his choicer remarks."

Shayne closed her eyes and whispered a Spanish prayer her Costa Rican nanny used to repeat each night to chase away the demons hiding under the bed. Of course, once she'd been taken to Florida, she'd had to say those prayers all on her own. Not that they'd worked. "Why is he upset that you married me?" she asked again.

"He's afraid you'll try and change things. He's sort of possessive about his kitchen."

Was that all? She felt instantly better, though she had trouble communicating that fact to her knees.

"Hey, you okay?" Chaz gathered her into his arms. "He won't hurt you. Honest."

If only she could believe that. And yet, with the heat from her husband's body stealing through her, tasting the taut length of his neck that she'd somehow found beneath her lips, inhaling his spicy cedar scent, she did feel safe. His hands snagged in her hair, tipping her head back. Fierce blue eyes focused on her with explosive need. He murmured something, something that sounded remarkably like "my love." But that couldn't be.

And then she couldn't think. His hands tangled deeper in her hair, forcing her up into a scalding meld of lips and tongues and heated breath. She slipped her hands beneath his shirt, reacquainting herself with the flesh embodiment of strength and power.

"Everything will work out," Chaz muttered against her mouth. He drank deeply once more, drugging her with his taste. "You'll see. I'll take care of it."

How typically male. He had a lot to learn about the woman he married, if he thought he could cut her out of the loop. "Is Mojo one of your secrets?"

"No."

*No?* "Now I'm really worried. I think we're overdo for a talk, don't you?"

The door to Chaz's office opened on her words and Doña Isabella appeared in the doorway. "I agree. We are long overdo for a talk," she announced, her raven-black gaze raking them both with sharp reprimand. "Do you intend to stand there all day cooing like love-sick turtledoves or do you plan to grace me with your presence sometime in the near future?"

"I'm so sorry," Shayne said. How could she have forgotten the Doña? Not that it took much thought. First Mojo and his meat cleaver and then Chaz's embrace. It was enough to make her forget everything else—even a woman as formidable as this. "We're coming right now."

"I apologize for keeping you waiting," Chaz said

as they took their seats. "I see Penny brought you coffee."

"It is cold."

"That's what happens when you don't drink it when it's hot."

"Doña Isabella prefers tea," Shayne hastened to interrupt.

"Funny. Last time she said she detested tea."

The Doña dismissed his comment with a sweep of her hand. "An old woman is permitted to change her mind. It is one of the few pleasures left her."

"Yeah, and you take to it like a duck to water, don't you?"

Laughter gleamed. "If you are asking whether I enjoy being difficult, the answer is yes. I enjoy it quite thoroughly."

"I can tell." He planted his hands on top of his desk. "Let's get down to it, shall we? You've met my wife. I've given you what you requested. Now give me what I want."

The Doña's mouth compressed, her thoughtful gaze settling on Shayne. "She is a lovely choice. I didn't expect you to show such wisdom."

"Then what's the problem?"

She sighed. "You haven't told her, have you?"

"I planned to tonight." His voice hardened. "You've jumped the gun a bit by showing up today."

"Tell her now."

His eyes flashed in warning. "Don't push me, old woman."

"Tell her now so I can be certain she won't leave you once she knows the truth."

"You have no right—"

Doña Isabella slammed her cane against the floor. "I have every right."

"Go ahead, Chaz," Shayne prompted. "If it will satisfy the Doña, get it out in the open."

"Honey, I really did plan to tell you," he explained regretfully. "Just not like this."

That meant it was bad. She took a deep breath and fought for calm. She'd spent most of her life practicing self-control, learning to hide her thoughts behind an impassive mask. The years she'd spent with her aunt had honed that skill. And after her aborted marriage to Chaz, when her brother's guilt had threatened to overwhelm them both, she'd worked hard to maintain a cheerful facade so he'd have peace. Whatever Chaz's secret, she'd greet it with calm acceptance.

"It's all right," she assured. "I told you before we married that I'd accept your secret. I meant what I said."

"Very well." He seemed to gather inward, as though drawing his emotions under tight control. "Doña Isabella has something I want."

"I gathered as much."

"In order to get it, I had to meet her demands. The first was that I acquire a house."

"And the other was a wife?"

"Yes."

"And in return, she'd give you…what?"

He hesitated for a split second, then said gently, "In return, she'd give me my daughter."

# CHAPTER FIVE

*To My Long-Lost Bride,*

*Another year has passed without you in my arms. How many has it been? Four? Four long, impossible years. How I miss you, my Forever Love. Are you still waiting for me? Or have you found another? That thought haunts me, twists me into knots so I can't think straight.*

*Was it only my imagination that made me believe we were joined that night, that we're two parts of one whole? Can you still picture me, see my face in misty dreams, as I see yours? Do you hear me, Shayne, as clearly as I hear you—your voice whispering on the night wind, calling with every birdsong at day's break, murmuring in the streams as spring breaks through winter's icy hold? Or am I nothing but a faded memory?*

*I'm losing you, my sweet. I can feel it. And I know if that happens, I'll also lose the part of me that you kept alive.*

*Come back to me! I need you.*

IT TOOK took every ounce of self-possession for Chaz to remain in his seat. He wanted to leap across the desk, gather Shayne in his arms and carry her off to his bedroom. To explain about his daughter in private, with a gentleness that might have helped ease the hurt somewhat. But Doña Isabella had forced the issue, had taken the timing out of his hands. And instead his newlywed wife sat as rigidly as the Doña, her chin set at a desperately proud angle, her eyes two huge, dark pools of anguish, her wide, lush mouth compressed to hide the slightest of quivers.

"What's her name?" she finally asked, her voice ripe with pain. "Your daughter, I mean."

"Sarita."

"It's a lovely name." She said it with a generous sincerity that left him helpless to respond. "How... how old is she?"

"Three last August."

"The same age as my nephew, Donato. And...and Sarita's mother?"

If this didn't end soon, Shayne would end up in tears. He refused to let that happen, refused to give the old woman the satisfaction of knowing how badly he'd hurt his wife with his silence. He stood and came around the desk. "We'll discuss that later. Well, Doña? Are you satisfied now?"

The woman recognized the double-edged question and inclined her head. "*Lo siento,* Señor McIntyre. My timing was unfortunate. I should have allowed you the opportunity to explain in your own way."

"Yes, you should have." He offered his hand. "I'll see you out."

"What about Sarita?" Shayne asked.

The Doña rose to her feet with Chaz's assistance, leaning heavily on her cane. "I'll bring her by at the end of the month for a visit."

He didn't like the sound of that. "You said—"

"You have done all I've asked, so far," the Doña interrupted tartly. "I do not expect the rest of my requests to cause you any great hardship."

"Requests...or demands?"

She shrugged. "I try always to be polite." Her cane shot out and she used it to maneuver him clear of her path, showing remarkable agility for someone so crippled up with arthritis. "You often make common courtesy a most difficult task."

"I aim to please," he sniped right back, though for Shayne's sake, he probably should attempt to curb his annoyance. "I don't suppose you'd care to list the rest of your demands so I know there's an actual end in sight. Or do you make them up as you go along?"

She didn't like that. Her remarkable eyes flashed with dark warning. "Use care, McIntyre. Sarita is not yet in your possession."

"She will be."

Doña Isabella paused in front of Shayne. "And what about you, *Señora*? Are you willing to accept Sarita as your own?"

Shayne didn't hesitate. "She *will* be my own."

Her words shook Chaz to the core. They implied a permanence he couldn't handle if he hoped to maintain a safe distance. It was his daughter he wanted, not a wife. Especially not a wife with a heart as soft as Shayne's. Only Sarita mattered. But even as he made the silent assertion, it echoed through his mind, sounding rife with desperation rather than ripe with certainty, mocking his conviction.

He fought to remind himself of the man he'd become. Once upon a time he might have had something to offer a woman like Shayne, when he was young and foolish and believed that love was a solution instead of a tribulation. But he no longer believed in such an emotion. Not in its purity, not in its goodness, and sure as hell not in its durability. Nine long, lonely years had cured him of that particular fantasy. What he knew of love was dark and painful, the emotion nothing more than a shadow that stole across a man's heart and snuffed his soul. If he kept Shayne for his wife, she'd discover that darkness, too, and he'd end up hurting her again—just as Rafe had warned.

"I want my daughter, Doña," Chaz interrupted. "I've been patient long enough. I've given you everything you've requested. You wanted me to provide a home for her. I have. You wanted a mother for her. Here she is."

"And now I wish to assure myself that this home you have purchased and this woman you have taken for a wife will be suitable for my Sarita."

"Don't push me, Isabella."

For a split second, her regal facade cracked, revealing an old woman's vulnerability. All pretense had been forcibly ripped away and her internal battle to do what was best for Sarita waged across a network of lines cut deep into a once handsome face. "She is my only female great-grandchild," she offered in a pained voice. "She is not a stray cat or a dog in need of a good home. If I decide you are unsuitable, I will return with her to Mexico. I can provide her with everything she requires there."

"Can you?" Something didn't ring true about the Doña's statement. "Then why did you come to me? Why tell me of her existence when your granddaughter went to such pains to keep me in the dark? You could have returned to Mexico with no one the wiser. So why ask me to take Sarita if you're capable of providing for her so well?"

She didn't reply. Instead, the battle ended and her face smoothed into an implacable mask. She turned and marched relentlessly across the office before pausing in the doorway. "Sarita is in need of some culture, if she is to live in such an isolated place," she announced. "We leave for San Francisco in the morning. I will return at the end of the month. And I shall be interested to see the progress your wife has made toward turning this house into a suitable home for my Sarita."

Shayne followed, slipping a hand beneath Isabella's arm. "I'll do my best." She opened the door and offered the sweetest of smiles. "Why don't I see you out?"

Doña Isabella inclined her head. "If that is your wish."

*Damn Shayne's kindness!* Chaz thrust a hand through his hair, thoroughly exasperated. Great. Just great. The woman who'd haunted him for more years than he cared to remember coupled with the woman who'd plagued him nonstop for the past three months. Nothing good could come out of that combination.

"Jumbo!" he roared.

With more speed than grace, Jumbo lumbered into the office. He was a massive man, his skin bronzed to a coppery sheen by a heritage as diverse as it was interesting. His instant response suggested he'd been hovering nearby. No doubt he'd gotten quite an earful, all of which he'd pass on word for excruciating word to his brother, Mojo, and to Penny, as well as to anyone else who'd pause long enough to listen. Jumbo might be one of Chaz's hardest-working employees, but he was also an inveterate gossip.

"You bellowed?"

"Get supper on the table. And make sure there's plenty of liquid refreshment, if you catch my drift."

"Aw, boss." Jumbo shook his head in disgust. He

folded arms that could have passed as tree trunks across his chest and lifted a single, thick black eyebrow that extended, unbroken, from one side of his face to the other. "You gonna drink yourself into a stupor on your wedding night?"

"It's not my wedding night." Or was it? Did their pre-wedding celebration count? Damn. Probably not. Nor did the overnight drive it took to get here. "And don't give me that look. I'm not the one in need of stupefying, not that it's any of your business."

A knowing gleam drifted into Jumbo's odd gold eyes. "Got it. Champagne for the lady? Or wine?"

"*Not* champagne." She'd probably kill him. "Wine. A nice merlot, I think. And keep her glass full, though I doubt it'll help." Nothing would help except to change the events of the past. Unfortunately, if his life had taken a different course, he wouldn't have Sarita. The knowledge unsettled him. "And keep Mojo in the kitchen. No point in scarin' my wife off her first day here."

"He'll want a peek at her."

"Tough."

"Okay, but fair warning. He might not be willing to cook for your wife, especially if she starts messin' around in his kitchen."

"We'll deal with that if it happens." Since Shayne might not be staying long enough to mess with anything, Chaz decided to back-burner that particular problem. Hell, he had enough other, far larger worries looming over him. "Now will you take care of your brother or do I have to do it?"

Jumbo held up his hands. "Don't sweat it. I'll deal with Mojo." And with that, he returned to the kitchen.

Offer her more wine," Jumbo advised.

Chaz shot his employee an infuriated look. Not that it did any good. The man was as immune to the finer points of authority hierarchies as Penny. He gritted his teeth. "More wine?" he asked Shayne.

"No, thanks."

"You sure? It's got quite a pleasant flav—"

"I'll pass, thank you."

Right. She'd pass. Again. Just like she'd passed on the salad, and the bread. And no doubt just like she'd pass on most of her dinner and Jumbo's eventual offer of dessert, and most frustrating of all, any and all attempts at conversation. He reached for the glass she'd refused, before slamming it to the table in sheer frustration. Purple-red wine sloshed over the rim and stained the one good tablecloth he could call his own. Good linen had never seemed important...until now.

"Shouldn't push her, boss," Jumbo advised cheerfully, dropping a dinner plate in front of him. "Maybe she doesn't like wine. If you're still hopin' to get her drunk, I can fetch some of that hard stuff you have hidden in your desk drawer. We could lace her coffee with it."

"Repeat that word."

Jumbo's face collapsed into lines of contemplation. "What word?"

"The 'b' word."

"What? Boss?"

"Yeah. That word. I want you to reflect on it and all its many connotations before opening your mouth again. That way you might keep your job past the end of the meal."

Jumbo's impressive eyebrow bunched together, like

a caterpillar rolling into a ball to escape a predator. "What? What did I say?"

"First, you're buttin' in where you have no business buttin'." Chaz fought to keep his voice down, with only limited success. "Second, you're giving out far too much information. And third, I'm *not* trying to get my wife drunk."

"Oh, yeah? You give up on that plan? Didn't much care for it, myself."

*"Jumbo!"*

Perhaps it was the volume that finally penetrated. "You want me to shut up?"

"Either you can do it, or I'll do it for you." Chaz flexed his hands, just in case.

Jumbo's caterpillar brow thrashed around in apparent death throes before rippling into a straight mortally wounded line. "Won't say another word."

"Good."

He set an overloaded dinner plate in front of Shayne. "Anything else I can get you?" He shot Chaz a defensive look. "And just so we're clear, I wasn't buttin' in. Asking her that is part of my job. Can't very well fetch her something if I don't know what needs fetching."

"No, thanks, Jumbo," Shayne hastened to say.

"But you're gonna eat all I brung you, right?"

Shayne blinked in surprise. "To be honest, I'm not very hungry."

Jumbo planted his massive fists on his equally massive hips. "Not a good idea."

Her eyes widened. "No?"

"Not even a little. If you kept this up, Mojo's gonna come charging out of the kitchen with a meat cleaver in hand, demanding retribution. He doesn't take well to people giving his food such short shrift."

"Jumbo!"

His employee spun around, his right elbow missing the top of Shayne's head by a scant inch. "Do you want your wife chopped into itty-bitty pieces, boss? I'm just trying to protect your property."

"She's *not* my property!" Chaz roared. What was it with people considering his wife property? First Rafe and now Jumbo. Couldn't they tell by looking at her that she was as strong and independent as they came? Perhaps it was because she appeared so fragile and was possibly the most delightful bit of femininity to ever grace his home. No doubt it roused the protective instincts in the male species. "She's a woman with a will of her own and the ability to make her own decisions."

"Now, see…" Jumbo took a seat. "There's your first mistake. You tell a woman stuff like that and things get way out of control."

"Jumbo's not the most enlightened of men," Chaz explained to his wife. "Perhaps that explains why he's never been married."

"You want my advice?" Jumbo asked. Not that it was really a question.

Chaz sighed. Clearly, he needed to redefine the word "employee" again. This time he'd do it with his fists. "Not even a little."

"When you went to that fancy-pants ball you should have bought yourself an obedient sort of wife. Not that there's anything wrong with the one you did buy. It's just that with a different sort, you could tell her straight out that she's to mind the house and take care of your kid and she wouldn't get her feelings hurt.''

"I did not buy a wife! I never said that.''

"Not in so many words,'' Jumbo concurred. "But we caught your drift.''

To his alarm, Shayne shoved back her chair and tossed her napkin to the table. Aw, hell. "Honey, I did *not* tell anyone I bought you. I swear.''

"Would 'barter' be a better word?'' Jumbo asked pensively. "You know... You agree on a trade-off. You give her a home, she gets to take care of it. That sort of thing.''

She shot to her feet. "Excuse me, please.''

Damn and double damn. "Honey, wait—''

She listened to him as well as everyone else in his household, doing precisely the opposite of what he requested. She didn't run, but she did move at a good little clip, hastening into the hallway and toward the bedrooms at the rear of the house. He'd lay odds that she was crying.

Chaz turned on his employee. "Have Mojo put together a light meal that'll keep. Then you stick it on a tray outside my bedroom door. And do it quietly, or I swear, you won't see another dawn.'' He slammed his finger into Jumbo's chest. "Tomorrow, you and I are going to conduct a little experiment.''

"What sort of experiment?'' Jumbo asked warily.

"We're going to experiment with how many times I can punch you in the jaw before all your teeth fall out.''

Not waiting for a reply, Chaz left the dining room and gave chase. He found his wife at the end of the hallway, looking around, clearly without a clue as to which door to try. He settled the issue by swinging her into his arms and carrying her into their bedroom. Twilight had settled in, bringing a deepening gloom. But when he reached for the light switch, she stayed his hand.

"Don't," she whispered.

Now he knew she'd been crying. Chaz fought for patience, fought to be the sort of man she deserved instead of the one she'd ended up marrying. "Honey, we have to talk."

Darkness filled her voice. "Not really."

"Yeah. Really."

"Then talk. But no lights."

"I can't see your reaction to what I say without lights," he argued.

"I know."

Okay, fine. They'd do this her way. All things considered, it seemed only fair. He settled her onto the bed before moving away, giving her a bit of space. He snagged a ladder-back chair from against the wall and brought it closer to the bed. Spinning it around, he straddled the seat and folded his arms along the back.

"I'm sorry, Shayne," he began. "First for the things Jumbo said. But also… I should have told you about Sarita before we married."

She curled up in the center of the mattress, hugging his pillow in a way that sent white-hot desire bolting through him. She'd hugged him like that the night of the Cinderella Ball. Of course then she'd been wearing only three things—a mask that sang of her desire, her petal-soft skin and the secret scent of a woman's passion.

"Why didn't you? Why keep Sarita a secret?"

"Because I was good and pi—" His wedding band caught the final rays of fast-dying light and he broke off, rethinking his language. The irony wasn't lost on him. Forty-eight hours ago, he'd have blistered the air with his opinion. Now he was learning the fine art of husbandly caution. Amazing. "I was good and ticked at your deception. I didn't feel I owed you a thing at that point, sure as hell not an explanation."

"I see." She lowered her head and her hair spilled forward, the deep reds and purples filling the evening sky catching in the pale gold color, like a molten sunset embracing a field of wheat.

"Look, Shayne. I know I hurt you. Not only didn't I tell you about Sarita. But I hurt you through the mere fact of my daughter's existence."

"We weren't married." She wrapped herself so tightly around the pillow it was a miracle the seams didn't burst. "You weren't under any obligation to remain faithful to me. I understand."

"Do you?" The question slipped out before he could stop it. But once spoken, he had to know the answer.

She tossed the pillow aside, as though throwing off a crutch. "I'm sure you'll find this hard to believe, but yes. I do understand." Even her voice had gained strength. "What you don't want to hear is why I understand."

No. He didn't. They were forbidden words, words that tied him in knots of restless anger and despair. "Her name was Madalena," he said with forceful deliberation. "And she made life a little easier during a tough time."

Shayne looked at him. Not that it did any good. Without any light to gauge her expression, it remained as unreadable as if she'd been wearing her mask. Even her voice held a cool, even quality that threatened his sanity. "Did you love her?"

"Do you really need me to answer that?"

"You don't think you're capable of loving anyone, do you?"

Her question whispered through the darkness, chilling him. Perhaps it was the lack of emotion in her voice. Or perhaps it was the quiet acceptance. He didn't want to hear either one. Cursing beneath his breath, he came for her, following the sweetest of scents with unerring accuracy.

He caught her in his arms, her small gasp revealing that she hadn't anticipated his approach. "I loved you once upon a time. Isn't that good enough?"

"No!" She fought him, shoving at his chest and squirming in a way that sent heat scalding through his veins. "You're afraid to live, Chaz. I wouldn't have thought it possible, but you are."

"Not afraid, wife," he whispered close to her mouth. "Cautious. Suspicious. And more than a little cynical."

She turned away from that almost-kiss, her rigidness spurning his touch. But he refused to release her. Or perhaps he simply didn't dare. "What happened to Madalena?" she asked when it became clear that he wouldn't let her go.

"It was a temporary diversion."

"For you or for her?"

"Both," he replied evenly. "She was the youngest in her family and a natural-born rebel. They tried to box her in and she fought back in the one way they couldn't forgive."

"Did her family find out about you?"

"Yes."

"And they took her from you, too?" She relaxed ever so slightly, turning into his warmth. "Oh, Chaz!"

He'd have laughed if it wasn't so tragic. "No, Shayne. They didn't react the way Rafe did. Their response wasn't loving outrage. They cut her off without a penny."

"They disowned her?" He could hear the shock ripple through her voice. "How could they?"

"Misplaced pride. Inflexibility. Who knows? The only one to stand by her was her grandmother, Doña Isabella."

"Couldn't you have done something to help? Couldn't you have married her?"

"I didn't know she'd been thrown out. Even if I had, Madalena didn't want marriage any more than she wanted me." He rested his chin on top of Shayne's head. "I told you. It was a temporary relationship. When it became apparent that our feelings for each other had changed, Madalena packed her bags and wished me well. Doña Isabella showed up the next day and they left. A week later, I moved on to my next job."

"They didn't tell you about Sarita?"

"Not then. Not until a few months ago. Doña Isabella dropped in to inform me that Madalena had died in a car accident. She brought Sarita with her."

"Quite a surprise. Or is that too mild a word?"

His mouth curved into a faint smile. "I think 'shock' might be closer to it."

"Isabella must have felt you should be told about your daughter. Why else would she have brought her?"

Shayne had keyed in on the one issue that didn't make any sense. "I'm still trying to figure that out. If Doña Isabella doesn't want me to have Sarita, why tell me about her? Why all the games?"

"I gather she offered to let you raise your daughter?"

"To adopt her. But only if I could provide a home for her."

"And a wife?" The hurt stormed back into Shayne's voice.

He released his breath in a sigh. "That, too."

She fell silent for a long moment and he felt the tension building in her, thrusting against his chest and arms, rejecting him with unspoken, yet clear determination. "Perhaps this would be a good time to discuss what you require from me," she said.

What the hell did that mean? "What the hell does that mean?"

"Jumbo wasn't far off, was he? We did make a bargain. You told me you wanted a wife who could create a home." She slipped from his grasp before he could stop her. "You just neglected to mention the home was for your daughter, rather than for us."

She was killing him by inches. "And?"

"And I'd like to know precisely what that involves. What do you want from me?" she repeated.

He didn't have a clue how to answer that one. Rolling off the bed, he crossed to his dresser and removed a T-shirt. "Here." He tossed her the improvised nightgown. "We're both exhausted and I don't know what Jumbo did with our suitcases. Wear this tonight and we can unpack tomorrow."

"I'm not sleeping here."

"Then pick another room. Doesn't matter much to me where we bed down."

"I mean... I'm not sleeping with you."

He'd already figured that out. Not that it altered his decision any. "We sleep together." He said it in a tone he rarely used, but one that made even the most ornery cowpoke scramble to obey. "Now get changed."

He thought he heard a word he'd have sworn his precious wife didn't know. Between that and the rustle of clothing being shed, he knew he'd won this particular battle. Trying to ignore the surge of relief that one argument had finally gone his way, Chaz opened the door and recovered the tray Jumbo had left. A shaft of light slipped into the room and as he turned, he saw Shayne.

She knelt in the center of his bed, her legs curled beneath her and her arms lifted as she prepared to drop his T-shirt over her head. She'd removed her clothes and the light licked across her profile. Time paused for a breath, gifting him with a second that seemed to last an eternity, enabling him to look his fill. Golden hair streamed down her back, the ends stopping just shy of the full, lush curves of her buttocks. Creamy thighs joined with narrow hips, shadows taunting him by throwing a modest hand across the golden delta beneath her flat belly. Her breasts were high and round, the rosy tips pearling in reaction to the cold kiss of the surrounding air. Her face was turned toward him, the vulnerability revealed in her wide, dark eyes burning a permanent path to his very soul.

He kicked the door closed, returning her to the protective embrace of the darkness. And then he fought to breath, to force air into badly depleted lungs. Desire clawed at him, demanding that he toss the tray aside and take the woman on his bed, to brand her with his possession.

"Chaz?"

Her voice slipped through the darkness, ripe with apprehension, and he knew that he couldn't do anything that would hurt her. He'd caused her enough pain. Fighting as he never had before, he slowly regained his self-control. Memory guided his footsteps to the end of the bed and he set the tray on the mattress.

"You didn't eat your dinner, so I had Jumbo leave this."

"You didn't eat, either."

He snapped on the bedside lamp. Shayne had retreated beneath the covers, the blankets pulled to her chin. He'd suspected that she'd been crying earlier and one look at her face confirmed it. Her lashes formed damp spikes and he could make out the faint track of dried tears on her cheeks. Helpless rage swept through him—anger at himself for provoking her tears and anger at her for opening herself up to hurt. If she'd just realize that love wasn't all it was cracked up to be, if she'd just deaden her emotions, life would be a hell of a lot simpler. They could take pleasure in each other's company without all the angst.

And without the guilt.

He recovered the tray and settled next to her. Mojo had put together a huge romaine salad liberally sprinkled with mesquite chicken, sweet red peppers and croutons. Chaz speared a sliver of chicken and fed it to his wife. She took it without protest, which was either a testament to her exhaustion or to her hunger. Whichever, he wasn't about to complain.

He waited until she'd eaten a decent-size portion of the salad and the crispy rolls before speaking. "Here's the deal, sweetheart.... I'll do anything to get my hands on my daughter. Unfortunately, Doña Isabella holds all the cards. If she decides to hightail it out of the country with Sarita, there's not much I can do about it. At least, not without a lengthy legal battle. I'd rather avoid that, if at all possible."

"And I'm the means by which you'll get Sarita." Her dark eyes were trained on him, filled with some unnamed and unwanted emotion. "That's why you married me, to gain custody of your daughter?"

He steeled himself to say the unforgivable. "That's about the size of it."

Her lashes swept downward, concealing the warmth of her gaze and shutting away feelings that shouldn't matter. So, why did her cool reserve annoy the hell out of him? Why was he tempted to catch her chin in his palm and force those beautiful brown eyes to look at him, to see if he could coax free the expression that had glittered there when they'd made love? He forced himself not to touch her, knowing he'd be unable to restrain himself if he were foolish enough to put his hands on her.

As though sensing his thoughts, Shayne wrestled the blanket closer to her chin. "You expect me to guess what the Doña wants and give it to her?"

"Yes. Though as to what that might be..." Desperate for something to do, he picked up the tray and dropped it onto the chair by the bed. "I gotta tell you, your guess is about as good as mine. Better, I'm willing to bet."

"Then you're giving me a free hand?"

Uh-oh. "Looks like I don't have a choice."

"And what happens once you have Sarita?"

He didn't pretend to misunderstand. "What happens to you?"

"Yes." She curled up against the pillow in a protective ball, small and vulnerable beneath the protective prickles of antagonism. "If I'm not pregnant and once you have custody of Sarita, what happens to me?"

# CHAPTER SIX

*To My Long-Lost Bride,*

*I've made a decision. It's a foolish one, I don't doubt that for a minute, but one I can't seem to resist.*

*Another Cinderella Ball is coming up and I've decided to attend one last time. I had a friend apply, so Ella wouldn't see my name on the guest list and warn your brother. But count on it. I'll be there.*

*I don't know. Maybe it's so I can say goodbye. Or maybe I'm just kidding myself and I'm hoping to find you again. Part of me expects to find you there. Strange, isn't it? After all these years?*

*I guess I need to know for sure. I need to be able to put you behind me once and for all and make a new start. I keep telling myself that even if you are there, we're not the same people we once were. There's a good chance that we'll take one look and run the other way.*

*But I have to know. I have to be certain that going forward in life without you at my side is the right thing to do. If you're there, we'll have another shot at it. Won't we, my Forever Love? And we'll take it.*

*If you're not there... I guess I'll have my answer, won't I?*

*Wait for me, wife. I'm coming.*

PREGNANT. Ripening with his child. The image was so strong, Chaz shook with it. "Why don't we wait and see?"

"No. I'd like an answer now." He could tell Shayne wasn't going to let go of this one until he responded. He'd never met a woman so determined to get herself hurt. "If I'm not pregnant, what happens to our marriage?" she repeated.

"Hell, sweetheart. I'm not going to throw you out."

"But you won't need me. You won't want me. Is that it?"

She had him good and cornered. "You're asking for answers I don't have." Naturally, he'd said the wrong thing. He'd managed to wound her again. Damn. He did some fast backpedaling. "If you're pregnant," he persisted doggedly, "then, of course, you stay."

It was still the wrong thing. "But only if I'm pregnant." Her mouth quivered, begging for a kiss he knew she'd reject. "If I'm not, the marriage ends."

"I didn't say that!" He closed his eyes, wishing he were one of those silver-tongued charmers who could spill lies as fast as a wild bronco spilled riders. "Honey, I'm so tired, I don't know what I'm saying. It's been at least two days since I got any shut-eye and you have to agree, today's been a bit of a trial."

His efforts to soothe must have lacked something. She rolled onto her side, confronting him with her back. "I think I'll go to sleep now. Maybe you should, too."

"Good idea." He stood and stripped off his clothes before joining her. He started to slip an arm beneath her shoulders, but she stopped him.

"We don't have to touch, do we? I don't think I

can—" Her voice broke, tearing him apart. "I think we'd sleep better if we didn't touch."

She was hurting, he reminded himself. And she was exhausted. The last two days hadn't been any easier on her than they'd been on him. "No. We don't have to touch," he assured gently.

"Okay. Good."

But it wasn't okay. He lay beside her and waited, waited until her hiccuped breath grew slow and steady and the tension fled her muscles. And then he rolled her over, easing her into his arms. Her hand slipped across his chest, settling close to his heart, and her head nestled into the crook of his shoulder. She curled up against him as though she'd done it a thousand times before, one leg thrown over the top of his, the soft probing of her knee giving him fits. He gritted his teeth, determined to endure.

But the final victory, the one that gave him peace enough to rest, came with the sleepy kiss she pressed against his jaw and the murmured words he shouldn't want to hear. Only then did he allow sleep to claim him.

Shayne awoke gradually, with the disconcerting realization that something wasn't quite right. She'd been warm and comfortable and lost in the most delicious of dreams—one she seemed to have been chasing for a lifetime. But it had vanished with the coming of morning…along with her heat source.

The clanging of a loud, brassy bell trembled through the room and Shayne pried her eyelids open. Chaz stood at the end of the mattress by the bedpost. As she watched, he slapped his Stetson on top of his head and aimed his penetrating blue gaze in her direction.

"Mornin'," he greeted warily.

He continued to stand there, rocking back on his heels as if he had all the time in the world. Apparently, he was waiting for her to respond. Considering the downhill slide their last conversation had taken, she wasn't too eager to start another. Still... She should try. "Did I hear a bell?"

"Just Mojo letting us know breakfast is ready." He hesitated, as though he had something more on his mind, but lacked the proper words to address it. "I'm sorry about last night," he said at last. "It wasn't quite the wedding night I'd planned for us. I'll—I'll try and do better."

"Better?" she managed.

"Yeah. Better." The muscles along his jaw knotted. "Less...less hurtful."

All that escaped her throat was a tiny squeak of disbelief. She must have looked a sight, her hair in a wild tangle, his T-shirt drooping off one shoulder, her eyes bulging, her mouth hanging open. He apparently took her mouse imitation as agreement, because he gave a nod of satisfaction and left the room. *Less hurtful?* What did that mean?

She remained in bed for a full five minutes mulling over his words, until it suddenly dawned on her that she'd been sleeping dab-smack in the center of the mattress. A slight depression remained where Chaz's body had been—a depression that she overlapped by a good foot. No question. At some point in the night, she'd slipped over to his side of the bed and turned him into a surrogate pillow and bed warmer. What she'd denied while awake, she'd revealed in her sleep.

*Less hurtful.* The words trailed her into the shower and around the room as she pulled clothes from the suitcase that had been dropped off at some point in the wee hours of the morning. It wasn't much, but it was a start. It meant Chaz was willing to try. A spark of hope sprang to life, a warm, determined glow lighting a path toward the future. Maybe, just maybe, their marriage had a chance.

Shayne found Chaz sitting in the dining room, nursing a cup of coffee. A second cup was steaming at the place setting next to his. She slid into the chair and buried her nose in the mug.

"So what are your plans for today?" he asked.

"I thought I'd figure out how to change this place into a home."

"Any ideas?"

Her nose dug deeper into the mug. "None."

"Don't panic. I'm sure something will come to you." He waited until she'd taken another couple sips of coffee before suggesting, "How about taking a day to familiarize yourself with the place? See if anything strikes your fancy. You might want to take a look at the bedrooms and choose one for Sarita."

He'd made an excellent suggestion. "How many employees can you spare to lend a hand once I'm ready to start?"

"You can have Jumbo. He turns his hand to most anything that needs doing around here. I'm down to the bare minimum of help, right now. But we can hire in town. There's always people looking for extra jobs before the holidays. Tell Jumbo what you want and he'll take care of it."

As though Chaz's comment had summoned him, Jumbo appeared in the doorway, two steaming plates in hand. "Mornin'," he said, greeting them with a wariness that made her smile.

They hadn't gotten off to the best start yesterday. Perhaps she could help them do a little better today. "Boy, I'm hungry," she announced.

Jumbo positively beamed. "Well, then, little lady. I have the perfect start for your day." He slapped a heaping platter in front of her. Beside her, Chaz snorted. "I have more if this isn't enough."

Her smile weakened. "Thanks. I think this will be plenty."

"Don't tease me now. This little ol' helpin' would hardly satisfy a gnat."

"No, really. It's plenty."

He clicked his tongue. "Mojo's gonna come out here, for sure," he warned sorrowfully. "Hope you weren't too partial to your wife, boss man."

"She's mine. I'm keeping her. And if Mojo wants to have words with me about it, I'll be happy to oblige."

Chaz's spirited defense perked her right up. Dropping her napkin into her lap, she won a grin from Jumbo by seizing her fork and tackling the mountain of scrambled eggs. It wasn't until she'd made a dent in one corner that she gave Chaz her attention again.

"I have my first request," she informed her husband.

"Yeah? What's that?"

"I want a dog. A big, hungry wolf of a dog."

His mouth eased into a broad smile. "And where would you like him, wife?"

"Right under my chair," she replied, returning his grin.

"I'll see what I can do."

Twenty minutes later, she shoved her plate away and groaned. "I can't eat another bite."

"But you're only halfway through. Mojo—"

"Mojo! And more Mojo. This is getting ridiculous." Tossing her napkin onto the table, she stood and started for the kitchen.

Chaz came after her. "Honey, this may not be a good idea."

"I think it's an excellent idea." She shoved open the door to the kitchen. Jumbo sat on a bar stool that fronted a huge, long counter. Standing at the sink, his back to her, was the giant of a man she recognized as the infamous Mojo. He made Jumbo look like a shrimp. "Hello," she said brightly.

Mojo's spine grew rigid. Apparently, with one simple word, she'd managed to say the exact wrong thing. "That the missus?" he asked his brother.

"Yeah. That's her."

"What does she want?"

"I don't know." Jumbo eyed Shayne. "What can we do for you, missy?"

"I though Mojo and I should become better acquainted."

"Mojo doesn't get acquainted."

Shayne folded her arms across her chest. "He does now."

Ever so carefully, Mojo set the frying pan he'd been cleaning on the draining board and wiped his hands on his apron. He turned, revealing a face slashed into pieces and just barely stitched back together again.

She didn't flinch as she suspected every other person confronted with Mojo's disfigurement did. Instead, she openly studied the vivid red scars. Then she crossed to his side. Ignoring the way he stiffened at her approach, she stood on tiptoe and pushed aside the thick black hair covering his brow, exposing a particularly nasty cut shaped like a lightning bolt. It split his brow in two before racing toward the corner of his eye.

"Boy, were you lucky," she commented. "A fraction of an inch lower and you could have done a great pirate imitation. Black patch, snarl and all. What happened? Car accident?"

"Let's just say my horse doesn't have a windshield anymore."

Shayne choked. *"Horse?"*

Jumbo chuckled. "It's a joke. Me and Mojo don't ride."

"Maybe because there isn't a horse born willing to carry you," Chaz offered from the sidelines.

Mojo scowled. "We get by with our Jeep."

Shayne managed to figure out the punch line on her own. "I assume you named your Jeep Horse?"

Jumbo looked impressed. "You got it. One day Horse decided to toss ol' Mojo on his face by running itself off a mountainside and into a big ol' spruce."

"That sounds familiar."

Shayne moved to the nearest countertop and lifted herself onto it. She peeked at her husband from beneath her lashes, wondering how he'd handle this next part. Well, he'd have found out sooner or later. Better sooner. Better still, she could show him her secret someplace where they weren't alone and he'd be forced to control his reactions. She unbuttoned the left sleeve of her blouse. While the men watched curiously, she rolled it up, exposing a faint, jagged scar of her own.

"It goes right up to my armpit," she announced. "I'm lucky I can still lift my arm. I still get odd tingles when the weather changes."

Chaz inhaled sharply and Shayne glanced his way, nerves strung taut. He looked gut-punched.

Mojo whistled. "Nice."

"That's nothing." She yanked the blouse from her the waistband of her jeans and revealed a network of silvery lines along her ribs. She managed a flippant grin. "I've got them all over this side of my body. I'd show you some more except my husband might object."

"What the hell happened?" Chaz demanded.

"Car accident. Same as Mojo."

"How? When?"

"A while ago, by the looks of them." Mojo came close enough to whistle over a few of the more impressive ones. "How long were you laid up?"

The question enabled her to evade her husband's shocked questions. "A couple months. Not including the cosmetic surgeries to get rid of some of the worst ones."

"Hah. Got you beat. Six months," Mojo boasted. "The first week I flat-lined three times. The doctors didn't think I had a chance."

"Yeah? Well, I lost half my blood volume."

"No!"

She grinned. "Okay. Maybe not half. But it was a lot. If my brother hadn't gotten to me so quickly, I'd have been a goner for sure."

Chaz's mouth had acquired an odd, white-lipped appearance. "Rafe was there?"

She chose her words with care. "He was following me at the time."

"Where?"

"Costa Rica. Those mountain roads can be really hazardous."

"Then we'll make sure you stay off the ones around here."

Relief vied with annoyance. "That'll be a little tough to do living in the shadow of the Rockies."

"You'll stay off them," he repeated in a voice he no doubt hoped would end the subject.

She simply shrugged and returned her attention to Mojo. "About the kitchen…"

The cook scowled. "What about it?"

"That seems to be an area of concern. Or so I understand."

He folded his arms across his massive chest. "You have something to tell me?"

"I sure do. Since I'm so busy revealing secrets today, I thought I'd reveal another."

"What's that?"

"I don't cook."

Mojo positively beamed. "No cooking? For real?"

"No cooking. For real. Our housekeeper in Costa Rica tried to teach me a number of times, but finally gave it up as a lost cause."

Chaz relaxed enough to smile. "How many dinners did you burn?"

"Too many to count. Rafe was amazingly equitable about the whole thing. Maybe because he'd just rescued me from—" Her mouth snapped closed an instant too late.

"Rescued you from…?" Chaz repeated softly. "Who? From me?"

"*No!* No," she repeated again, so there wouldn't be any doubt. "You know full well I didn't need rescuing from you."

"Then who?"

"My…my aunt." She hopped off the counter and

offered his employees a brilliant smile. "So have we resolved the kitchen crisis? You'll continue cooking for us, Mojo?"

"You got it. And if there's something special you want some night. Well, hell. I'll even consider fixing it."

"I appreciate the offer," Shayne said gravely. "And I'll try not to take you up on it."

He patted her on the back, his meaty hand nearly leveling her. "I knew I liked you. A bit on the scrawny side, but I can take care of that."

Chaz stepped in before Mojo pounded her into the ground with his enthusiasm. "She's fine how she is."

"Not if she's eating for two."

Chaz whipped around. "What did you say?"

"I have the eye," Mojo insisted proudly. "Got it from my momma. She could see things like that and so can I."

Shayne caught Chaz's hand and tugged him toward the door. "Come on. Mojo's just teasing. It's too early to know for sure."

He allowed himself to be drawn from the kitchen. "Mojo's gonna find himself out of a job if he's not careful."

"Trust me. You don't want to do that."

He cocked an eyebrow. "Oh, yeah? You really that bad?"

"Worse." She shot him a grim look. "Far, far worse."

"But, you don't understand, boss."

Chaz didn't look up from his accounting book. "There's nothing *to* understand, Jumbo. She's in charge. If she says to move something to the left, you damn well pick up the house by the foundations and move it to the left. Got it?''

"But... But she has a *clipboard*."

That caught Chaz's attention. "A what?"

"You heard me. It's one of those official ones with a pen hangin' from it and..." Jumbo's single eyebrow knotted into a ferocious scowl. "And it gets worse. I don't know how to tell you this, boss. So I'm gonna come right out and say it. But I want you to brace yourself."

Aw, hell. "I'm braced."

"She's makin' a list. Just like she was Santa freakin' Claus."

Chaz put down his pencil. "A list, you say?"

"Don't that beat all?" Jumbo began to pace, eating up the huge room in three short strides. He turned and rumbled toward the desk again. "It wasn't very nice of me, but I peeked at the damned thing. And it's numbered and everything."

Chaz ran a hand across his jaw. "Numbered." He shook his head. "That sounds serious."

Jumbo planted massive fists on his equally massive hips and glared, his eyebrow doing a mambo from one side of his face to the other. "Whatcha gonna do?"

"Looks like I'll have to talk to her. Any idea where she is?"

"In one of the bedrooms." He shuddered. "I'll just wait here until you turn her from the devil's spawn back into that sweet little lady you married."

"I'll get right on it."

Chaz ran her to ground in the spare bedroom he'd considered using for Sarita. His wife was curled up on the padded bench in the bow window that overlooked the pasture, cradling something in her arms. Tossed to one side was the clipboard with its ominous list and he couldn't help but grin. She'd even changed for the role she'd taken on, dressing in neat black wool slacks, crisp black blouse and power jacket. And she'd tortured that glorious hair into a businesslike knot.

He came up behind her and made short work of the knot, allowing the straight, pale strands to slide free. Then he slipped his hands beneath the golden waterfall and massaged the stiffness from her neck. "I didn't think it was possible, but you actually scared Jumbo."

She kept her back to him, leaning against his chest and staring out at the snow-peaked Rockies. "So I gathered. I suspect it was the clipboard that put him over the edge."

"He's in my office trembling like a scolded puppy. I'm standing here prayin' he doesn't wet the carpet."

A hint of laughter touched her voice. "I'm sorry. I was just trying to be organized."

"Do me a favor, will you? Try a little less organization so you don't chase off the help." She nodded in agreement and he asked, "Come up with any brilliant ideas?"

"A few." She straightened away from him. Ever so gently she took the box she held and set it on the window seat next to her. "I decided this would be the perfect room for Sarita. I gather you did, too."

Damn. He'd forgotten he'd left that here.

Shayne turned the box around, revealing the doll he'd bought Sarita, the sort he hoped a little girl would find irresistible. The face was porcelain, the hair long with shiny black curls. She was dressed all in satin and lace, her dress poofed out over layers and layers of petticoats. Long silky lashes framed big brown eyes that stared solemnly up at him.

He cleared his throat, aware that something had gone terribly wrong, but not quite sure what or why. "I heard little girls like dolls that share their coloring."

Shayne closed her eyes, suddenly exhausted. How could a man who acted with such thought and care think himself so heartless? It didn't make sense. "It's absolutely gorgeous," she said. "Sarita will love it."

"Will she? I picked it up for a Christmas present or as a little special something to make her feel more at home when she moves in here. What do you think?"

It was the first time she'd ever heard him sound uncertain. He must want his daughter very badly. Part of her rejoiced for him, that he'd go to such lengths to make a home for her. But another, far less noble part, wept that he'd never made such an effort for his long-ago wife. She collected her clipboard and stood. "I think it's the perfect present, whenever you choose to give it to her."

He caught her arm as she started past. "Have I done something wrong?"

"No, of course not."

"You're upset. Why?" He studied her intently. "Is it this clipboard business?"

"Don't be ridiculous."

"Is it because of last night? Are you afraid I'm going to dump you once I have Sarita?"

She didn't have the energy for another confrontation. How could she explain to a man who didn't believe in love that she'd spent her entire life searching for it? That once upon a time, she'd found it in his arms. And how could she explain to a man who didn't believe in love that it was the one thing his daughter would crave more than anything in the world, including beautiful, porcelain-faced dolls? Shayne had once been a little girl who'd lost her parents, and been left in a cold, sterile environment without love or laughter or reassurance. They'd been the worst years of her life, a full decade that had left scars more permanent then the ones she carried on her body. As a result, she'd learned that, without love, life was a wasteland.

She stared up into her husband's eyes, those gorgeous blue eyes that could be as hard and cold as a winter's day one minute, and gentle and concerned and brimming with kindness the next. Right now they were summer-warm. *Are you afraid I'm going to dump you once I have Sarita?* he'd asked. Didn't he understand?

"No, Chaz. I'm not afraid of that." She fought to keep her mouth from trembling, to reveal how heart-wrenching she found their situation. "I'm afraid—terrified, actually—that you're serious. That you really don't know how to love, anymore."

And as she watched, winter descended, sweeping into the harsh lines bracketing his mouth and darkening the sunshine of his gaze. "No need to be afraid of the truth, honey," he said, coupling his exaggerated accent with a humorless smile. "Just face right on up to it."

# CHAPTER SEVEN

*To My Long-Lost Bride,*

*I went to the Christmas Ball. It goes without saying that you didn't.*

*I don't know what to write anymore. I don't know what to feel. I guess that's because there aren't any feelings left. I never thought I'd give up. But right now...*

*I met someone, Shayne. I don't love her, but then, I don't think I'm capable of experiencing love anymore. Madalena and I have reached an understanding and she seems happy enough, even though I don't have much to give her. Hell, if I were honest, I'd admit I don't have anything to give her, not that she's asking. But she fills a void that's grown larger with each passing year. A void I suspect will someday consume me.*

*So why do I feel like I'm cheating on you?*

*I've failed you, honey, and I'm truly sorry for that. But this is it. I can't take anymore. And so, my long-lost bride, I'm saying a final goodbye.*

*If I could have found a Forever Love, it would have been with you.*

CHAZ remembered the exact second the realization struck. He was on a ladder, pulling all manner of debris out of the gutters around the house. *He could have lost her.*

He'd spent years searching for Shayne and she

could have been permanently lost to him ages ago, killed in a car accident on a twisty mountain road in Costa Rica. And he'd never have known of her fate. Despite the frigid temperatures, he broke out in a cold sweat. He climbed off the ladder before he fell off and walked into the house. He found her upstairs, ordering the general destruction of all three spare bedrooms.

She paused mid-order and looked at him, an eyebrow raised in question. "Do you need something?"

"Yeah," he said roughly. "I do."

He waved the workers from the room, then stripped off his work gloves and dropped them to the floor. The second they were alone, he backed her up against the nearest wall and cupped her face in his hands. For a long moment, he simply looked at her, drinking in the delicate features. She had such soft, creamy skin, the healthy flush of exertion highlighting her arching cheekbones. As he watched, she moistened her full, lush mouth and fixed him with velvety dark eyes. Eyes that had haunted him for years. Eyes that continued to haunt him even when he stood perched on a ladder, cleaning out gutters.

"Chaz?" she whispered.

"Shh. I just had to do this."

"Do what?"

Words escaped him so he let his actions answer instead. He slipped his hand around the nape of her neck and drew her up toward his mouth. And then he tumbled into sheer pleasure, the fall long and hard and endless. But it wasn't painful. Not when he was caught by the most delectable set of lips he'd ever kissed. He inhaled her, consumed her, ate her up in quick, hungry bites.

*She could have died.*

But she hadn't and the evidence was lifting on tip-toe to return his embrace. His fears subsided, if not his desire. If anything, his desire had become so strong, he could barely think straight. He scooped her closer, relishing the feel of her soft breasts flattening against his chest and the rounded hips snuggling into the cradle of his. If there hadn't been people nearby, he'd have taken her then and there. Would she have wrapped her slender legs around him and allowed the wild storms to consume them? Or would modesty have prevailed? Their passion deepened with flash-burn intensity and he had his answer.

But how long would that passion last? How many days would he continue to crave the woman in his arms? How long would it be before his heartlessness destroyed their marriage? How many nights would pass before one or both of them became sated into dissatisfaction? He kissed her again, harder and more uncontrolled this time, desperate to hold the future at bay and focus on the delights of the moment. She was harbored safe within his arms—if his arms could be deemed a safe harbor. Not that Shayne seemed to share his doubts.

For his wife, his sweet, precious wife, gave her mouth with such unstinting tenderness and generosity, so open to his every desire, that it threatened to utterly destroy him.

If she lived to be a hundred she'd never understand the man. "I don't understand you, Chaz. I thought you wanted me to fix the place up."

"Yes. Fix it." His jaw worked in an odd way. "Fix means paint. Fix means doodads on the furniture. Fix means...means—" His arms made a few pinwheels in the air. "It means a rug here and there and maybe one or two of those useless colored pillows. It doesn't mean *this*!''

"I wasn't going to leave the bathroom without plumbing for long. I just had to pick fixtures more suitable to a little girl.''

"Little girls need railings on their tub?''

She avoided his gaze. "And in the shower. Along with one of those cute seats in the corner. They're perfect for holding all the shampoo bottles. Little girls use *lots* of different shampoo bottles. A whole seat covered with them.''

He crammed his Stetson further down on his brow and clamped his back teeth together. "Fine. Have a shower with a seat. But *two* sinks? What does she need two for?''

"Yes, well...'' Inspiration struck. "It's obvious you've never had a house full of females before.''

"One little girl is *not* a house full of females.''

"It is when she has friends over for her birthday or a slumber party.''

Chaz paled. "Slumber party?''

"They're essential,'' Shayne stated firmly. At least, they had been for the girls she'd gone to school with. Her aunt had never allowed her to attend any, let alone throw one, so her knowledge of sleep overs was painfully limited. But even so... "Why, as soon as word gets out that you have a daughter, I suspect you'll be overrun with hordes of little girls.''

"Hordes,'' he repeated faintly.

"Giggling and shrieking and putting on makeup.''

For the first time in her entire life, she saw Chaz look downright terrified. "Makeup? Sarita's only three!''

"They do grow up fast,'' she replied cheerfully.

"No." He shook his head. "Oh, no. Not my daughter."

She wrinkled her brow in thought. "I seem to remember Rafe saying something similar about me. Except it was in Spanish and there was some sort of threat involving the first man who tried to date his little sister."

Chaz slumped against the wall in defeat. "Date?" he croaked.

She patted his arm. "We'll talk later. Right now I have a meeting with the electrician. Little girls need lots of electrical outlets for their stereo systems and electrical outlets for their private phone lines." Giving his arm a final pat, she started down the hallway. "Now, what did I do with my clipboard? I really should make a few notes so I don't forget to arrange for the satellite TV hookup."

"What the *hell* happened to my floor?" Chaz roared.

Jumbo held up his hands in surrender. "Don't look at me. This was all your wife's idea."

"My—" He should have known. "And just where is my dear wife?"

"In your office."

Chaz frowned. That didn't make him any happier. A man's office should be sacrosanct, even from wives. He jabbed Jumbo's chest with his finger. "Don't cut any more holes in my floor. Got it?"

"Sorry, boss," Jumbo replied cheerfully. "I'm not taking orders from you these days, remember? You told me to do everything Shayne said and that's what I'm doing. Including six more holes."

A growl of frustration rumbled deep in Chaz's

chest. "Keep it up, big man, and I'll have you riding fence line until your...your ears freeze off."

"My ears, huh?" Jumbo whistled. "Marriage sure has done strange things to your grasp of the English language. You aren't anywhere near as colorful as you used to be."

The fact that his employee was right only served to aggravate Chaz all the more. "Oh, yeah? Well, your colorful days will soon come to a screeching halt, too, my friend. The second my daughter hits this house, I don't want to hear a single word not meant for a child. And that goes for Mojo, too."

Jumbo grinned. "You gonna tell him that or you wanna tie a note to a rock and heave it in the general direction of the kitchen?"

Momentary laughter glittered in Chaz's eyes. "Think I'll let my wife handle that particular duty."

"And he'll take it like a lamb. Hell, he'll probably even smile at the scolding." Jumbo shook his head in disgust. "Never thought I'd see the day when a woman would lead my little brother around by the...er...ears."

"You haven't seen anything, yet. Wait until my daughter moves in. She'll have him tied up and put in his place within the hour."

Assuming she moved in. Which brought him right back to Shayne. Chaz glanced at the door to his office—a closed door. A closed door behind which sat his precious wife getting into heaven only knew what sort of mischief. Dammit it all, he had work to do. He couldn't afford to spend all his time—

Giving in to the inevitable, he thrust open the office door. "Shayne, what the hell have you done to my floors?" he demanded.

She sat behind his desk, her glorious mane of hair once again constrained in a painfully tight knot at the nape of her neck. His hands itched to ease the tightness, just as he longed to ease her toward their bedroom and kiss his way down all those silvery scars. Of course, he hadn't been given the opportunity.

The only time she'd allowed his touch in the past two weeks had been the far too infrequent kisses they'd exchanged during the day or when she'd been sound asleep. Only then would she curl into his arms and wrap herself around him. Only then would she kiss his jaw and whisper her forbidden words of love, allowing him to join her in sweet oblivion. Only then did he find true peace. Their marriage was killing him, bit by bit, chipping him into pieces he'd never be able to put together again. Not that his wife noticed. Hell, no. She remained frustratingly oblivious.

Glancing up from the papers scattered across the oak surface of his desk, she cupped a hand over the phone receiver. "I'll be with you in a minute."

"We need to talk, Shayne—"

Of course, she ignored him. "The ones I want are all three foot square and labeled FT dash one through twelve. Could you have them crated and shipped to me? Air express the package, if necessary. Yes, I know it'll be expensive, but send them anyway. See they get through customs yourself, Chelita. Or have Marvin take care of it. He'll make sure there's no hang-up. He and I have an understanding."

Say, what? "Who are you talking to?" he demanded. And what the hell kind of an understanding did his wife have with a Marvin?

"Thanks, Chelita. Talk to you soon."

He didn't wait for her to hang up. "Who the hell is Marvin?"

"A friend. He grew up in the village outside Rafe's coffee *finca*."

"And what is he bringing through customs?"

"Some of my artwork."

"Oh." Damn. Here he'd worked up a good bluster and she'd managed to drain it right out of him. He switched to a different subject, one that would allow him to bluster all he wanted. "Now, look. About my floors—"

The door opened and a man with a tool belt dragging his pants in the general direction of his knees walked in. Swearing beneath his breath, Chaz shifted to block the worst from Shayne's sight. Dammit all! Here was something else he'd have to take care of before returning to work. Couldn't have some strange man wandering around like that in full view of his wife. It wasn't proper. And he'd make sure the fella knew it, too.

Shayne shifted her chair so she could see around him. "Hi, Tim. What can I do for you?"

"Punched those holes in the walls you wanted. No problem." He hitched his pants up. They stayed for a whole two seconds before gravity tugged them downward again. Another inch and serious action would be needed. "But would you mind taking a look before I frame it up?"

"Wait one damn minute here," Chaz interrupted. "Not *more* holes!"

Shayne gave Tim a smile that Chaz would have killed for, full and natural and tastier than anything Mojo had ever dreamed of serving up. "Thanks, Tim. I'll be right there." The door banged closed and she glanced at him, her smile fading. "I thought you put me in charge of the house."

"I did. But—"

She cut him off. "I don't recall their being a 'but' as part of our agreement. You said I was in charge and when you said it, there was a period at the end of your statement."

"I'm fairly certain I shoved a 'but' in there someplace," he retorted through gritted teeth. "Along with a comma so I could make amendments should someone put holes in my house!"

"You're shouting."

"I'm allowed to shout." He began to pace, needing some outlet for his energy other than snatching his wife out from behind that desk and giving full rein to every physical expression he could think of. Considering how long it had been since he'd physically expressed himself, he could think of a goodly number. "And I'm allowed to swear. And I'm allowed to complain like hell when my wife entertains half-naked men."

"You can't mean Tim."

He whipped around to confront her. "Yes, I mean Tim! If his pants drooped any lower you'd know him better than his doctor. You're supposed to be getting the place ready for my daughter. We only have a couple short weeks before Satan's sister sweeps in on her broomstick."

She tilted her head to one side. "Now there's an interesting image."

Chaz slammed his Stetson onto the desk, biting back some of the choicer words burning a strip off his tongue. "You know what I mean. Instead of fixin' stuff, you're ripping it down around our—our—"

His wedding band flashed a warning. Dammit all! Enough was enough. His life wasn't his own, anymore. His employees had turned traitor, his wife treated him like an annoying little brother, and he couldn't speak his mind without checking each word before he uttered it. But worse of all, he had an ache that wouldn't go away.

Well, there was one thing he could do. He could march out to the barn, oust the dang animals from their dang stalls, and turn it into a cussin' room. A place for men only and the fouler-mouthed, the better. No women. No holes in the walls. And no watching his language. Hell. He'd stick a refrigerator in there and stock it with beer and have himself more than just a room. He'd have a whole cussing *bar*. Of course, he'd have to put a lock on the damned place or his spread would be overrun with drunken cowboys.

Shayne lifted an eyebrow. "You were saying? I've been ripping the house down around our..."

He balled his hands into fists. "Around our *ears*."

"That's what I thought you were going to say."

She stood and circled the desk. To his everlasting disgust, she ended their argument by cheating. She wrapped her arms around his waist and slid every female inch she possessed along every male counterpart she could find. She said something else, but he didn't have a clue what it was. He was too busy dealing with far more serious problems.

At her first touch, every piece of hardware in his body went into instant overload. Massive system failure followed. Autonomic systems short-circuited and his brain shut down in an effort to recalibrate. He fought to breathe. Only one system remained on-line and in excellent working order. Her hip bumped it, threatening him with the very real possibility of total annihilation.

"Don't. Do. That."

She pulled back and looked up at him with a puzzled expression. "Is something wrong?"

Aside from the fact that he felt like he'd just been poleaxed? His jaw moved in an effort to imitate speech. She waited patiently, blinking wide brown eyes at him which forced him to recalibrate a few more brain cells. Maybe if he didn't look, he'd summon an answer to her question. It was there somewhere. Just one simple word. All he had to do was force the air from his lungs and the word from his mouth. "No."

"Okay." She gave him another brain-splintering hug and then trotted toward the door. "I'm going to check with Tim. Catch you later."

He didn't know how long he stood there. But when mobility returned, he used it to stagger in the general direction of the barn. The frigid winter temperature knocked him to his knees, but he had the air blistered nice and hot in no time, the curses sliding off his tongue faster than rainwater off a grease-dipped duck. If his wranglers thought his behavior at all strange, they were too smart to say anything. All except Penny, who swaggered over.

"Gotcha where it hurts, don't she, boy? Wives sure are good at that. Or so I've heard." He braved Chaz's wrath with a knowing smirk, then risked his neck further by adding, "Never been stupid enough to find out, myself."

"Okay, this is it. This is where I draw the line."

Shayne blinked up at Chaz in confusion. From her

kneeling position on the office carpet he managed to loom as impressively as Jumbo. "What line?"

"The one I'm drawing right here, this very minute." He shoved his Stetson to the back of his head and folded his arms across his chest. "Now, I didn't fuss about your tearing apart one of our bathrooms, which I think is damned decent of me. I barely said a word about that crazed electrician, even though I should have had him arrested for indecent exposure. And I've been the most understanding man in the world about the holes you've punched in the walls and in my floor."

"You have?"

"I've taken it like a lamb. And honey, that's saying a lot in cattle country." He gazed at her with such earnest sincerity, she was forced to accept he truly believed every word he'd uttered. "Why, there's not another man on this planet who would put up with the general mayhem goin' on around here the way I have without losin' his cool and banging a few heads together."

"There's not?"

"No way." He turned to scowl at her latest efforts on his behalf. "But this is going too far."

She looked around in bewilderment. "If it's because I'm using your office floor, it won't be for much longer."

"I can't get to my desk."

"I can." She half rose. "Is there something you needed? I'd be happy to get it for—"

"That's not my point." She sank back onto her heels as he gestured to indicate the strings of fairy lights gaily twinkling in neat lines on the carpet. "This looks suspiciously like Christmas."

Her brows drew together. His tone sounded utterly outraged, as though she'd committed some horrible sin. "That's because it is for Christmas. I thought I'd put up a few lights and decorations before—"

"Not in my house you're not."

"I'm not?"

"Not a chance in this world or the next. I don't do Christmas."

She stared at him, nonplussed. "What do you mean you don't *do* it?"

He ticked off on his fingers. "No lights. No tree. No silly ceramic angels or Santas cluttering up the place. No ribbons or bows or anything remotely red or green." He paused to consider. "Unless it's eatable. Don't want to be unreasonable about this. But no Christmas. Got it?"

"No."

Anger crackled in his eyes, intensifying the blue. "Come again?"

"You heard me."

Before matters could escalate further, Jumbo appeared in the doorway carrying an armful of tangled outdoor lights. He looked from Chaz to her and groaned. "Uh-oh."

Shayne turned to him for confirmation. "Boss man says he doesn't do Christmas. What's going on?"

His eyes widened and he shuffled his feet, practically tearing the carpet loose at the seams. "I couldn't say. I just work here, ma'am."

"You *can't* say…or you won't?" She gave him her sternest look. "Come on, Jumbo. Spill it. No Christmas? Not ever?"

His eyebrow began twitching nervously. "'Fraid not. Leastwise, not as long as I've known him and that's going on five years. He usually locks himself in his office with a bottle of Jack Daniels and a stack of writing paper and drinks himself into a stupor.''

Chaz whipped his Stetson off his head and slammed it to the floor. *''Jumbo!''*

The tangle of lights tumbled from his massive arms. ''What? What did I say wrong this time?''

''If I want my wife to know about my little fling with JD, I'll damn well tell her myself.'' He jammed his finger into the Schwarzenegger-like chest. ''Don't forget who signs your paycheck or it'll be my pleasure to remind you.''

''Shoot, boss. You keep forgettin' you assigned me to her. I *have* to answer her questions.''

Time to interrupt before blood got spilled, Shayne decided. She rose to stand nose-to-chest with her husband and did a little finger-jabbing of her own. ''And my next question is… Why do you dislike Christmas so much? Would you care to respond to that or shall I take it up with Jumbo?''

He didn't want to answer, Shayne could tell. The reason escaped her, though she'd get to the bottom of it eventually. He could be darned closemouthed when he chose. But then… She could be darned stubborn. He glared at Jumbo and jerked his head toward the door. Sounding remarkably similar to a herd of cattle in full stampede, Jumbo bolted from the office.

''Spill it, Chaz. What's going on?''

''If you have to know the truth, Christmas holds some bad memories for me,'' he confessed.

At one point in her life, it had for Shayne, too. All the more reason to replace the bad with some good ones. ''Is it anything you can tell me about?'' she asked sympathetically.

His jaw set. "I'm sorry, Shayne. I'm not ready to do that."

She fought to conceal her hurt, reminding herself that the "why" of his refusal wasn't as important as getting him to change his mind about the decorations. "Chaz, I can understand your reluctance, but surely you must see that you can't avoid celebrating Christmas. It's not fair to Sarita."

Lines sank into his face and his gaze turned flat and hard. "Don't bring my daughter into this."

She wouldn't give up. Even if it meant suffering his wrath, she'd push him on this to the bitter end. "Do you really think you can simply ignore the season into nonexistence?"

He gave a callous shrug. "Works for me."

"Well, it doesn't work for me. Nor will it work for Sarita. And I guarantee it won't work for Doña Isabella."

"Considering that the Doña won't be around come Christmas, what she doesn't know won't hurt her."

"And me? Will I still be here? Or don't my wishes count, either?"

"Whether or not you're still here hasn't been determined, yet. Are you pregnant?"

His hard-edged question took her breath away, the reminder delivered with all the brutality of a backhanded slap. She fought against the tears burning for release. This wasn't the man she'd married nine years ago, she tried to tell herself. Circumstances had replaced him with the stranger standing before her, one with a heart as frozen as the peaks outside her bedroom window. What in the world had happened? What had caused him to become so cold and remote...and what could she do to coax free the Chaz she'd married all those years ago?

It took a full minute to regain control enough to speak. "I don't know whether or not I'm pregnant," she lied.

He held onto his coolness for a moment longer, then seemed to thaw ever so slightly. "I'm sorry, Shayne. That was uncalled for."

"Is Christmas when Madalena left you?" she asked gently. "Is that why it holds such bad memories?"

She half expected him to freeze her out again. Instead, he shook his head. "This doesn't have anything to do with Madalena. I don't like the season. End of subject."

"So that's it? That's your final word?"

"That's my final word."

## CHAPTER EIGHT

*To My Long-Lost Bride,*
*    I can't even begin to explain why I'm writing to you again this year. Habit? Or am I just a glutton for punishment? I don't love you. I don't. I don't love anyone, anymore. What feelings I had died long ago.*
*    But still I look at other women and think...*
*They're not you.*
*    Shayne... What happened to our Forever Love? Why can't I get you out of my mind?*

"WHAT part of my final word...as in *no* Christmas... didn't you understand?" Chaz roared.

Shayne sat perched high on a ladder placed dabsmack in the middle of the hallway, clutching streams of ivy to her chest. She blinked down at him with the most innocent expression he'd ever seen. Too bad he didn't believe any part of it—not the thick, fluttering lashes that surrounded killer fudge-brown eyes, not the lush, moist lips parted with such innocent seduction. And certainly not the spine-tingling, husky way she said, "Whatever do you mean?"

"You know damn well what I mean." He swept his arm through the air to indicate the latest changes to his surroundings-dramatic changes that seemed to come faster with each day that passed. "These Christmas decorations. The ones I said you weren't to bring into my...er...our house."

133

"*Our* house?"

His altered phrasing elicited a delicious smile, one that melted him for a whole two seconds before he remembered why he was so flat-out furious with her. "That smile isn't going to cut it, sweet stuff. Now, I want all these decorations out of here. Pronto."

"Don't be silly, Chaz. These aren't for Christmas," those lush lips lied with brazen disregard.

"You have twinkly lights up! If that's not—"

"Oh, that." She dismissed them with a wave of her hand. "Those aren't Christmas lights."

His jaw worked. "They're not."

"Goodness, no. Would you like to know how I can tell?"

"Please. Tell me." Reining in his anger, he folded his arms across his chest and braced his shoulder against the doorway leading to the dining room. "This I've gotta hear."

With blatant disregard to her personal safety, she wriggled her pert little bottom more firmly onto the top step of the folding ladder, not showing the least concern when the aluminum legs wobbled alarmingly beneath her. "See, Christmas lights are red, green or white. These are blushing tea rose pink."

"Blushing tea rose pink."

"Exactly. And those bows? The ones holding up the ivy?" To his relief, she stopped squirming around, reducing the ladder's wobble to a mild shimmy. "Well, they're not Christmas bows, either."

He ground his teeth, amazed they weren't down to useless stumps by now. "No, of course they aren't. Let me guess. That's because they're purple."

"Don't be ridiculous. They're puce. And I haven't

used any pinecones or greenery or mistletoe or anything remotely Christmaslike.''

He pointed to the garland of ivy twisting a graceful
path around his door frames. ''So, what do you call
that stuff?''

''Cosmetic work. You said I was supposed to take
care of that, right? Heck, the ivy isn't even green.''

''Then what is it? Salamander red?''

She chuckled. ''Now you're teasing. You know perfectly well it's blue. Bluegrass pine, to be exact.''

''Are you trying to tell me the 'pine' and 'grass'
part aren't green?''

''Not even a little.'' She swiped her arm in an ex-
pansive gesture, nearly tipping herself over backward.
''The blue overrides any other color.''

''Uh-huh.'' He straightened away from the door
frame and approached her ladder. ''First, when I said
no Christmas decorations, that's what I meant. And
that includes all this stuff. Second, when I asked you
to oversee the cosmetic work, I meant for you to slap
a coat of paint on the walls, not drape ivy all over the
place. And third, if you don't fill in the holes in the
floor soon, someone's libel to fall in and never be
found again.''

The ladder trembled rather violently. ''There's a
subfloor,'' she explained. ''It's not likely anyone will
fall through that.''

''No, they'll just trip and break something.''

''You know...'' Strands of ivy fluttered from her
hands, snaking affectionately around his boots. ''It's
funny you should mention the holes. Jumbo will have
them taken care of by the end of the day.''

''Would you care to tell me how Jumbo will take
care of it?''

She cleared her throat. "I think I'll leave that as a surprise."

He frowned. Reaching up, he plucked her off the ladder before she fell off and set her in front of him. She stood there, her expression so full of hope, he found it painful to witness. "And will it be as much of a surprise as your un-Christmas decorations?"

"Count on it."

"I was afraid you'd say that." He leaned down and carefully untwined the strands of ivy from around his ankles before he found himself nose-down in one of Shayne's holes. As tempted as he was to rip the garland apart, he didn't think he could face her expression if he accidentally damaged it. Winding the garland into a neat coil, he set it aside. Then he eyed the twinkling fairy lights—the tea rose blush pink twinkling fairy lights—the puce-purple bows and blue ivy that looked amazingly green to his eyes. "Honey, I hate to tell you this, but it's all got to go."

Her soft mouth quivered in a way he longed to ease with a kiss so hard and time-consuming it would wipe every other thought from her head. "But...*why*?"

Before he could explain even one of his objections, a knock sounded at the front door. No doubt sensing a reprieve, Shayne darted around him and tugged it open. Doña Isabella filled the doorway. And hovering at her side, her tiny hand clinging to the Doña's, stood his daughter. She gazed at them with huge, apprehensive eyes, shrinking closer to her great-grandmother.

Shayne greeted them with a huge grin. "Doña Isabella. What a pleasant surprise." She stooped to the little girl's level. "And this must be Sarita. Hello, sweetie."

Sarita buried her face against the old woman's

skirts, then peeked at them, the prettiest smile Chaz had ever seen slipping free.

The Doña looked around inquisitively. "I hope we haven't arrived at an inconvenient time."

"How can it be inconvenient since I'm sure you planned it that way?" Chaz asked dryly.

Shayne chuckled. "You just ignore him. It's not inconvenient at all." She threw the door wide and gestured for them to enter. "Now don't trip on the holes in the floor. We'll have those covered up before the end of the day."

The cane paused mid-tap. "Holes in the floor?"

"You know... That's just what Chaz said when he first saw them. Of course, he said it a bit louder."

"Shayne!"

"Just like that, as a matter of fact."

Sarita tugged on her great-grandmother's hand and pointed to Shayne's latest "cosmetic" contributions to his house. *"Abuelita, mira! Qué bonita."*

*Abuelita?* Chaz fought to suppress a grin, with only limited success. Somehow he'd never pictured anyone having the nerve to call the austere Doña Isabella "little grandmother." But apparently his baby girl was an exception. One look at his nemesis, however, killed his grin dead.

Once she deemed him appropriately cut down to size by her razor-sharp glare, she turned her attention to their surroundings. "What beautiful Christmas decorations," she commented with admirable sincerity. "You have done a lovely job."

Shayne shot Chaz an uneasy glance before addressing their guest. "Oh, they're not for Christmas. Goodness, no. I just thought they looked pretty. But if you notice, I didn't use any Christmas colors, which means they're not..."

She trailed off dispiritedly and Chaz felt like an utter heel. She'd worked so hard to get the place spruced up and ready. And all for his daughter, all so he'd be granted custody by the black vulture hovering beside Sarita. He gave in to the inevitable. "Glad you like it. Shayne deserves all the credit. She's worked hard on making the place perfect for the holidays. I assume you're here for the grand tour?"

"If it wouldn't be an imposition."

"Now why would you think that?" he asked dryly.

"How about if I show you around?" Shayne hastened to suggest. "That way you can make suggestions for any changes that occur to you."

Doña Isabella graciously inclined her head. "That would be acceptable."

"Great! Where would you like to start?"

"Have you prepared a bedroom for Sarita?"

"That was my first project. Come this way." She stuck her hand behind her back and waved Chaz off. Then she held out that same hand to Sarita. His daughter spared him a brief, wistful glance, before slipping her fingers into Shayne's and trotting down the hall with the two women. To his dismay, that single look squeezed something he thought long dead. Chaz closed his eyes. He really needed to do something about opening up that cussin' bar. Right now he had the overwhelming urge to cuss up a storm while swigging down a gulp or two of rotgut—anything to ease the unexpected pain centered in a forgotten place deep in his chest.

"Keep in mind that we can change the colors of the walls if you don't care for them," Shayne offered as she led the way deeper into the far recesses of the house. "And the furniture can be replaced, too."

"You are very accommodating," Doña Isabella murmured.

Something in the woman's tone caught Shayne's attention and a small frown etched a path across her brow. "You make that sound like it's a bad thing."

"It could be, if it's not sincere."

Shayne pushed open the door to the room she'd prepared for Sarita and waited until the little girl was preoccupied exploring her surrounds before turning to the Doña. "I'll make you a promise, Isabella," she stated with quiet conviction. "I'll never lie to you. And I'll never pretend to feel something I don't. I'll also treat that little girl as if I'd brought her into this world myself. She'll never have a moment's doubt that she's both loved and wanted. And she'll never, ever be made to think she's a burden."

"A burden?" Doña Isabella's eyebrows drew together over her hooked nose. "What an odd suggestion. Explain where it comes from."

Shayne didn't want to answer, but gaining this woman's trust and understanding was paramount. Reluctantly, she opened a small part of her soul that she'd rather have kept far from prying eyes. "I lost my parents when I was three. My aunt raised me."

"It was not a successful relationship?" Doña Isabella asked delicately.

It took a full minute before Shayne could reply. "My brother, Rafe, rescued me when I was thirteen."

"I see." No doubt she did, too. Doña Isabella hadn't lived so many years without witnessing what life had to offer, both for good and ill. "And you will see to it that my Sarita does not share your fate?"

"You have my word."

For a long moment, hard black eyes held her, boring straight through to her heart. And then the Doña inclined her head. "I believe you." Turning her attention to the bedroom, she sighed with pleasure. "This is quite lovely."

Shayne had worked hard on the room, trying to turn it into a safe retreat for a little girl. Feeling safe when you're torn from the only family you'd ever known was important. Even after all these years, she still remembered that. She'd chosen creamy white furniture to match the soft wool carpet. The walls were a sunny yellow with the bedding in yellow and white pinstripes trimmed in Swiss lace. She'd also gone out of her way to provide lidded boxes in bright colors and secret cubbyholes for storing private treasures. But what had instantly captured Sarita's attention was the doll propped up on the window seat. She'd not dared to touch, but instead had knelt beside the box, staring with great dark, hungry eyes.

Shayne joined her on the window seat. "Your daddy bought that for you. Would you like to open it?"

With an excited nod, Sarita picked up the box and carefully pried open the lid. The packaging defeated her, so Shayne gave her a hand. From that point on, the doll never left Sarita's arms, the object of periodic hugs and whispered conversations.

Shayne indicated a door on the far side of the room. "There's a bathroom that opens onto an adjoining bedroom," she explained to the Doña, before pointing out the huge walk-in closet to Sarita. "If you go in there, you'll find a secret tunnel hidden in the far back.

Why don't you crawl through and we'll meet you on the other side?''

Doña Isabella lifted an eyebrow in question. ''We will take another route, I trust?''

''We'll go through the bathroom,'' Shayne reassured with an understanding smile. ''You can make sure the fixtures are acceptable.''

The Doña's keen gaze didn't miss a thing about the way the plumbing had been set up. And though she lifted an eyebrow in question at some of the features Shayne had chosen, she contained her curiosity. Tapping her way into the second bedroom, she looked around, wordless.

Facing south, the room embraced the sunlight, glowing with vibrant gemstone colors. Although Shayne had wanted to use a thick, luxurious carpet that could be difficult for people with canes, so she'd settled for a short, tight weave that wouldn't catch at unwary feet. But she'd compensated for the loss with the accessories, making them rich in texture and restful to the eye. The bed and dresser only took up a small portion of the room. Against one wall, she'd set a cozy love seat, perfect for snuggling with a little girl and in another section, a roomy ''play area'' with comfortable chairs, an inlaid wooden card table and a small entertainment center.

Shayne shot Doña Isabella a quick, nervous glance, before erupting into speech. ''There's a private phone line and your own TV with a satellite hookup—the cable companies refuse to run their lines this far—so you can watch Oprah or the soaps or one of the Spanish channels. Since this room is larger than Sarita's, I've put an itty-bitty kitchenette in one corner, in case you don't care for Mojo's cooking. Though, my goodness, he's quite a wonder with a skillet. Just don't let his face scare you the first time you see it. He's a little sensitive." She pointed to a long, blank wall, begging for some pictures and chattered on. "Maybe this spring I can convince Chaz to poke a hole in the wall over there for a door and build you a small outdoor patio. He's sort of funny about poking holes in the walls, but don't let that worry you. We can also add on a private bath, if you'd rather not share. Now, there is a third spare bedroom which has its own, but that's further away from Sarita and right next to our bedroom. It's more of a nursery, if you catch my drift. So, I thought... I thought this room would be best."

Doña Isabella waited until she'd run out of air before asking, "You designed this for me?"

Shayne twisted her hands together. "I understand you probably have relatives clamoring for you to live with them back in Mexico. But I also know how it is to lose the one person you love most in the world. It would make Sarita happy if you stayed." She couldn't tell how the Doña was taking the offer. "Or if you must go, we can keep this room for whenever you visit."

Sarita poked her head out of the walk-in closet. Seeing them, she beamed. "*Abuelita!* I came through the tunnel."

Doña Isabella stared at a point just above the wrought-iron headboard of the bed. "What is this tunnel?"

"Oh, that." Shayne looped a strand of hand behind her ear. "You see, the closets were back-to-back, so I had a passageway knocked through so they'd connect.

That way Sarita could slip in for a visit whenever she wanted.''

Tears filled Doña Isabella's eyes. "You did this for me?" she whispered. "You truly wish me to stay?"

Shayne didn't hesitate. "Yes, please. I think family's important and you're all Sarita has left of her mother.''

The old woman fought for composure. "McIntyre will not approve.''

"Oh, well. We'll just tell him it's temporary until he gets used to the idea.''

"That may take quite a while.''

"He'll come around. He pretends he's heartless, but his heart's in there somewhere.'' It had to be. "We'll root around until we find it. What do you say? Want to help?''

A single tear followed the network of lines down Doña Isabella's face, though a fierce, innate pride kept her from breaking down completely. "It may be interesting to remain, if for its amusement factor, alone.''

Uh-oh. That didn't sound good. "Perhaps you won't mind if I break the news to him?''

A hint of laughter replaced Isabella's tears. "I would like to be a fly in the wall for that conversation.''

Shayne grinned. "Somehow I suspect I'm the one who'll be in the wall.''

Gnarled fingers reached out to touch Shayne's cheek and the Doña murmured softly in Spanish, "Are you very certain you want to do this, child?''

"Quite certain,'' she replied in the same language, wondering how the Doña knew she was fluent. Perhaps Rafe wasn't the only one capable of hiring a private investigator. Considering how protective the Doña was of Sarita's well-being, Shayne could see her taking every possible precaution. "I'm in charge of creating a home. I wouldn't be doing a proper job, if that home didn't include you. Please stay with us. Chaz doesn't realize it, yet, but we need you."

"Walk me to the front door, if you will." Doña Isabella tucked her hand into the crook of Shayne's arm and signaled to Sarita who obediently followed, whispering secrets to her new doll. "You may tell Señor McIntyre I have agreed to let him have custody of his daughter. Perhaps that will ease his anger a trifle when he learns the rest. Tell him also that until I'm satisfied that my great-granddaughter is properly settled, I will stay for a visit."

"An indefinite visit."

"Yes." Isabella broke down and smiled—a smile of unexpected beauty. "Most definitely indefinite."

They found Jumbo in the hallway, carefully filling one of the holes in the floor with the first of the mosaic squares she'd had shipped from Costa Rica. It was from a set of twelve, each a depiction of one of the months of the year. Beside her, Isabella drew an astonished breath. "Where did you get this piece?" she asked, still speaking in Spanish.

"I made it."

Isabella stilled. "You are an artisan?"

"In my spare time."

"And your name before you married?"

"Shayne Beaumont."

"I have seen your work, Shayne Beaumont. There was a mosaic piece I viewed quite recently..." Her brow drew together and she rapped her cane sharply against the floor. "But of course. On loan to the museum in San Francisco. It was quite striking. A man, half in darkness, half in light.''

"It took me quite a while to create that one. To be honest, I didn't think I'd ever finish it. But, I have to admit, it's my very favorite.''

"Does your husband know?''

Shayne shook her head. "And I'd rather it stayed that way, if you don't mind.''

Isabella shrugged without offering any promises. "I remember thinking at the time that the man reminded me of someone. Now I realize who. The resemblance to McIntyre is quite striking.''

"Thank you.''

"I was a foolish old woman not to see it before.'' Doña Isabella's eyes narrowed, as something else occurred to her. "You said this work took you a while to create. How long a while might that be?''

"I worked on it sporadically over an eight-year period. At one point I gave up on it altogether. But my sister-in-law helped me through some tough times and encouraged me to finish what I'd started.''

"Then...'' Isabella released her breath in a gusty sigh. "You knew McIntyre long ago. Before my Madalena came into his life.''

"We were briefly married,'' Shayne confessed, wondering how the Doña would receive the news. "But my brother thought I was too young and had it annulled.''

"This explains much that I did not understand.''

Apprehension filled her. "Has it changed your mind about coming to live with us?''

"No, my dear.'' To Shayne's delight, Doña Isabella leaned forward and embraced her. "It has proven to me that I made the right decision. But you should tell your husband about this artwork and allow him to judge it for himself.''

"I can't."

"Because it is too revealing," Doña Isabella guessed shrewdly. "It is sad to see two people so much in love and so afraid to show it."

"You're wrong! Chaz doesn't love me."

Isabella regarded her with open amusement. "When you are as old as I, you will see the folly of your words, as well as this decision regarding your artwork. And when you do, you will either laugh with your husband over your foolishness. Or..."

"Or?" Shayne prompted, dreading the response.

"Or you will cry in your lonely bed, filled with regrets that come far too late." And with that, she took Sarita's hand in hers and tapped her way to the front door.

"What do you mean she's left? Where's Sarita?" Chaz shot from behind his desk, ready to chase them down. Dammit all, he'd drag the old crow back by her hooked nose, if necessary. In fact, he half hoped it would be. "I...I didn't even get the chance to say goodbye."

"It's all right," Shayne attempted to soothe. "She'll be back."

"What did the witch tell you? Will she let us have Sarita?"

"Pretty much."

"Pretty much? What the hell does that mean?" He thrust a hand through his hair, his gut twisting at his wife's sudden nervousness. "Let me guess. More conditions?"

"Just one. I promise, it's the last."

"I'd feel better if *she* promised it was the last." He propped his hip onto the corner of his desk and fought to control his impatience. Over the past month, he'd found that particular skill more and more difficult to master. "Let's have it, sweetheart. What's the catch?"

To his concern, she wandered toward the far end of his office where a large picture window faced out the front of the house. "This would be a perfect place for a Christmas tree," she murmured.

"We already had that discussion, remember?"

She wrapped her arms around her waist, looking suddenly small and alone. "I was hoping you'd changed your mind."

"Not even a little."

"But Sarita—"

"Forget about the damn tree, Shayne, and tell me what the Doña wants."

She turned, taking unfair advantage of his soft nature by allowing huge, glittering tears to fill her eyes. "She's a child, Chaz. She doesn't understand that you have some personal reason for hating Christmas. All she knows is that she's alone and without family—at least family she recognizes—and it's Christmas. Only there's no music and no laughter, no tree or presents."

He straightened and cautiously approached. There was something going on here, something that escaped him. "Why do I have the funny feeling we aren't talking about Sarita, anymore?"

She paled and he knew he'd struck a nerve. "I...I'm sorry." She clasped her hands in front of her and tilted her head to look directly at him. Her chin quivered in a way that twisted him into knots, but she didn't back down, refusing to give in to her distress. "You're not the only one who has bad memories of past Christmases. But I'd never take them out on a child. I'd do everything I could to give her happy experiences, hoping that they'd give them to me, as well.''

He reached for her with a gentle hand and brushed away a tear that had tumbled loose. ''What happened to you, sweetheart? Why all this commotion over a silly tree?''

''I just want Sarita to be happy.''

His eyes narrowed. ''I don't think so. Why is it so important for you to decorate the house? Come on. Spill it.''

The quiver had spread to her sweet, vulnerable mouth. ''I—I'm not feeling well. I think I'll go lie down for a little while.''

''Honey—''

She shook her head, backing away from his outstretched hand. ''Please, Chaz. Give me a little time alone.''

''Wait a minute. We need to talk. You haven't told me about the Doña's condition. And dammit all, Shayne, I want to discuss this Christmas business with you.''

''I don't think I can.'' Her voice broke. ''Not right now.''

With that she turned and fled the room. Every instinct he possessed urged him to give chase, not to wait until she'd had time to deal with whatever demons haunted her, but instead force them into the open. He hesitated, suspecting he was listening to raging male hormones, the sort that wanted to sweep her into his arms and fight those demons for her, instead of the more rational part of his brain that urged him to abide by her wishes.

He checked his watch. One hour. He'd give her one hour and then they were going to have a long talk about their past and about Sarita, about their marriage and about their future.

And then he'd give in to those raging male hormones.

# CHAPTER NINE

*To My Long-Lost Bride,*

*Another year has gone and winter has arrived again. Or has it always been here? Sometimes it feels that way. I look outside and see a blanket of white as beautiful and untouched as you were the first time we kissed. So many years have passed and yet the memories haven't dimmed.*

*I don't understand that. Our love died long ago, the embers long since turned to ash. And yet I look out my window and there you are, as clear to me as the first time I saw you in the Montagues' garden.*

*You'll stay in my thoughts, wife of my heart, a sweet memory I'll allow myself to recall just once a year. You linger in the far recesses of my mind. A laughter-filled voice. A tantalizing scent. A heart-stopping smile.*

*I'm keeping you there, where you'll be safe, where we can visit in my yearly dream, where you remain…my wife from long ago, the only one I've ever loved. A Forever Love.*

CHAZ eventually found his wife in their bedroom, curled up on the mattress, fully clothed and sound asleep. An hour had come and gone long ago, but an emergency with one of his animals had intruded.

Gazing down at Shayne, he wondered again why she'd been so upset earlier. He frowned over the pro-

150

tective way her arms were folded, the fetal position she'd assumed, and the slight reddening of her nose. And suddenly he knew the truth beyond any shred of doubt. He sank onto the edge of the bed. She'd discovered she wasn't pregnant and thought it meant a fast end to their short marriage. That's why she hadn't told him, because she'd suspected he'd send her away. He sat there for a long time, struggling to understand the disappointment that ate at him. He didn't want more complications in his life, did he? And yet...

A soft knock sounded on the door and Chaz opened it, surprised to find Mojo standing there, holding an overloaded tray. "The little missy just picked at her dinner, so I thought I'd drop this off," the cook explained with an abashed expression. "Maybe you can get her to eat something."

It amazed Chaz to realize how quickly she'd found a place in the hearts of his men. But then... Hadn't he tumbled just as hard at their first meeting? "I'll see what I can do," he promised.

Taking the tray, he set it on the dresser and glanced at his wife. She looked frighteningly vulnerable, adrift in the center of their mattress. Perhaps he'd slip her into a nightgown. If she woke, he'd feed her as he had their first evening together. Only this time, he'd try not to make her cry. For some strange reason, her tears worked him into an uproar, something he'd prefer to avoid, if at all possible. He opened one of the dresser drawers he'd cleared out for her use, intent on finding the briefest scrap of nightwear he could find.

The drawer was empty.

What the hell? One after another, he yanked them open, finding every last one bare. For a horrifying moment he thought she'd decided to leave him. That instead of telling him she wasn't pregnant, she'd just go. Fury gripped him. This was all Isabella's fault! She'd agreed to turn over his daughter and Shayne had taken that to mean he didn't need her anymore and packed her bags. Only one thing had kept her from disappearing into the night. She'd fallen asleep before she could make good her escape.

He crossed to the closet and ripped open the doors. A single dress hung there, but it was enough to loosen the fistlike knot that had formed in his chest. And then he saw it. Shoved off to one side on the floor of the closet he found her suitcase. Bits and pieces of silken underclothes spilled haphazardly over the side and she'd draped a knit shirt on top. The clothes were in reasonable order, but something about the way they'd been pushed around told him they weren't packed in anticipation of a hasty departure. A frown pulled his eyebrows together as understanding slowly dawned.

*She'd never unpacked.*

For one full month she'd lived out of her suitcase and he'd never even noticed. His breath expelled in an audible hiss. He knew what it meant. She'd known practically from the start that she didn't carry his child. This was her silent acceptance of the impermanence of their marriage. Her unstated fatalism nearly brought him to his knees. She planned to leave. Not today. But sooner or later, she'd neaten those bits and pieces of silk and lace, zip up her case and he'd lose her, just as he had all those years ago. Only this time it would be permanent.

*No. No way.*

He didn't know when it had happened, but at some point in the past few weeks, he'd gone from wanting a swift end to his marriage, to wanting to keep her with him forever. Not that he loved her, he assured himself. Hell, no. He wasn't capable of loving anyone. But she'd gotten...comfortable to be with. Convenient to have around. Necessary in some inexplicable way. Not that he'd tell her that. Like as not, she'd take it the wrong way. Either she'd be insulted or she'd read more into his declaration than he'd intended.

He stared at the bed with hungry eyes. Maybe he could give a gentle hint, tell her without words how he felt.

The idea appealed immensely. Removing the suitcase from the closet, he carried it to the ladder-back chair and set it on the seat. The sun had given way to dusk and he wouldn't be able to see for much longer without switching on a light. But he didn't want to wake Shayne until he'd finished.

Quietly, he opened the drawer to the nightstand table and removed the matches stocked there. Winter storms frequently knocked out the power and the first time he'd fumbled for a flashlight and found the batteries dead, he'd made a habit of keeping a hurricane lamp filled and ready. He lit the wick and turned it low. The soft glow barely kissed the small mound Shayne made in the middle of the bed. Satisfied that it wouldn't disturb her, he turned his attention to the suitcase.

Yanking open the first dresser drawer, he loaded it with delicate scraps of temptation. He stood there for a full minute trying to decide whether he'd be considered perverted if he folded her female fripperies instead of leaving them in a jumbled heap of pastels. Gingerly, he sorted the pile, not quite folding, but carefully arranging the tiny scraps into sections based on usage. That finished, he made short work of the rest, either stacking the articles of clothing into a drawer or hanging them in the closet, the decision based solely on its wrinkle-ability. At the very bottom of the suitcase, he found the mask she'd worn to the Cinderella Ball.

The bells greeted him with happy, silvered voices. Lifting his Stetson off the top of the bedpost, he draped the mask there, slapping his hat on top. The combination of hat and beaded mask made him grin. Then he turned and eyed the suitcase, his amusement fading. He picked it up and crossed to the nearest window. Shoving up the sash, he sent the case hurtling out into the frigid night air, taking a perverse delight in his actions.

"Chaz?" Shayne lifted onto one elbow, blinking at him with huge sleepy eyes. "Was that my suitcase you just threw out the window?"

"Yup." Supreme satisfaction edged his voice.

She sat up, shoving a tumble of pale hair from her face, looking quite delightful in her confusion. "But... Why did you do that?"

"I was making a statement." He crossed to the dresser and picked up the tray and placed it near her on the mattress. "Hungry?"

"I don't understand." She drew her knees toward her chest and wrapped her arms around her legs. "What sort of statement?"

"You're a smart woman. You figure it out."

Her lashes flickered downward, then lifted. An expression every bit as hungry as his lit the darkness of her gaze. "Should I assume I won't be going anywhere soon?"

"Good guess."

"Even though Isabella will let Sarita stay? Even

though you won't need me much longer? Even though... Even though we don't know for sure whether or not I'm pregnant?"

Oh, he knew. And he intended to take that excuse away from her right this very second. "I'm changing the conditions of our marriage agreement." He thrust out his jaw. "Any objections?"

"To be honest," she admitted wistfully. "I sort of liked the clothes I had in my suitcase."

"I didn't throw out your clothes, just the case." To prove his point, he opened one of the drawers and removed a particularly fine bit of black silk. If he were honest, he'd admit he'd had a few perverted thoughts about this particular piece of nothing while putting it away. With any luck at all, he'd turn those thoughts into action. "See? All your belongings, safe and sound."

Safe and sound until he ripped them off her.

"You know this doesn't change anything, don't you?"

Returning to the bed, he removed the plastic wrap covering one of the plates. He passed her the sandwich Mojo had prepared and waited until she'd begun nibbling on it before continuing. "This place needs a bit of work, but it's in a good location and has serious possibilities. I've worked on some of the ranches around here before and like the area. This is where I want to raise my daughter. The people are friendly and the town wholesome."

Shayne slanted him a quick glance from beneath her lashes. "Are you trying to sell me on the place?"

*She planned to leave him.* The certainty took hold. "Do I need to?"

"It occurs to me that we've never settled certain

issues." She picked at her sandwich, scattering crumbs across the spread. If their conversation hadn't turned so serious, he'd have teased her about it. "Maybe we should discuss them now."

He didn't want her telling him about the baby she wouldn't bear. Not tonight. "And maybe we should take things one day at a time."

A flash of pain flickered across her face and she returned her sandwich to the plate, half-eaten. "Did you ever look for me, Chaz?"

Damn. Where had that come from? He didn't have the energy for this sort of discussion. "I looked," he stated briefly.

"But Rafe made it impossible for you to find me, didn't he?"

He thrust a hand through his hair. "Do we have to talk about this now?" He didn't want to open old wounds, to discover whether or not anything still festered there. Some matters were best left untouched. It was safer that way. "I looked. I didn't find you. End of subject."

"How long did you look?"

"Shayne—"

"A day?"

A ripple of anger raced through him. "Let it go, honey."

"A month?"

"Yes, damn it. A month."

"A year? Did you keep looking for a whole year?"

Each question sliced deep, ripping toward that dark, bitter place, a place he didn't dare touch. "You don't know anything about it, Shayne," His tone was too low, too harsh. Too close to the edge. *She was going to leave him.* He had to get her to stop before he did or said something he'd regret, before he drove her away. He forced a deadly note in his voice. "Be smart. Drop it. Now."

"Was it longer than a year? Or did those twelve months pretty much cover it?"

"Did you hear? Stop!"

Her dark eyes flashed with a contradictory mixture of velvety softness and sharp reprimand, as though her emotions were at war with her reason. "You gave up, didn't you?"

For an instant he didn't move. A distant roaring filled his head, preluding the coming of an anger so deep and so old and so relentless that it drowned out every other feeling or consideration. He exploded from the bed, the bells on her mask startled into a frantic jumble of sound. Rational thought vanished, the thin veneer of civilization stripped away and replaced with sheer animal rage. With a guttural shout, he snatched the tray from the bed and threw it with every ounce of strength toward the nearest wall. Dishes shattered.

He caught a glimpse of himself in the mirror over the dresser and flinched. For what he saw was a man reduced to his most primitive state. Vivid color scored his cheekbones, the wild glitter in his eyes fired by deadly intent. Even the atmosphere in the room had changed, burning with the scent of fury, as though ancient pheromones had been released, igniting the urge to attack. He sucked air into his lungs, desperate to regain his control, shaking with the effort.

"I searched, damn you!" The raw words howled from a bottomless well of pain. "He bought off my private investigators. I sent you letters. You never answered. Where were you, Shayne? Why didn't *you* come to *me*."

"I came." She approached, adorable, foolish woman, braving his wrath with gentle hands and soothing words. "At least, I tried to."

The coldness returned, sweeping over him and he welcomed it. Embraced it. Clung to it. It would protect him from feelings he refused to acknowledge. "What stopped you, Shayne?" He turned on her like a wounded animal, intent on inflicting as much damage as possible before giving in to his own agony. "What possible excuse could you have?"

"I..." Sadness shadowed her expression. "I had a small accident."

He discovered in that moment that he had a heart and that this woman controlled its every beat. "An accident," he repeated stupidly. An accident. *The* accident.

He shook his head. No. Not that. Not the car wreck that had scarred that sweet, beautiful body. Not while she'd been coming to him. Not the one she'd told Mojo about, all the while shooting him quick, nervous glances, as though half-expecting him to reject her because of a few scars.

"I did that to you?" he whispered. "Your scars were my fault?"

"No!" She was in his arms, wrapping him in warmth. "It wasn't anyone's fault. It was a freak storm and a small rock slide on a bad corner. I lost control of the car."

"Rafe. He was trying to stop you, wasn't he?"

"He wasn't chasing me, if that's what you were thinking. He'd discovered where I was going and planned to intercept me at the airport. I was lucky, Chaz. If he hadn't come down the mountain when he had—"

*"Don't!"*

She broke off, pulling back ever so slightly. "You're shaking!"

"You're damned right I am." In one swift movement, he yanked her knit shirt over her head and tossed it aside. "And in a minute, you will be, too."

Her bra came next, neatly removed with a flick of his fingers. As much as he wanted to fill his hands with her softness, he had more important duties to take care of first—like getting her naked and on the bed where he could feast on her at his leisure. Unfastening her slacks, he worked his thumbs into the waistband and tugged everything that wasn't skin off her legs.

In less than thirty seconds, he had her exactly as he wanted her, the way he'd fantasized since that first passionate encounter before their wedding. Hell, if he were honest he'd admit it was a desperate memory he'd clung to for nine long years. Sweeping her into his arms, he carried her to the bed. He set her down, her body barely denting the mattress. She stared up at him without a hint of shyness and he found he appreciated that calm, direct gaze, relieved that her scars hadn't stolen that from her, hadn't filled her with self-loathing or embarrassment.

The instant his clothes hit the floor, he joined her on the bed. The kerosene lamp filled the room with shadows, but now that he knew what to look for, he found the network of scars with ease. Before this night ended, he'd kiss the full length of each and every one. They were a testament to his history with Shayne, to what they'd gone through to finally come together again. They were a silvery road map that had led to this moment in time.

"Chaz..." Her voice slipped through the dusk, filling him with longing.

How he wished he could love her as she deserved. That the deadness inside him would burgeon with new life. That the heart he'd just discovered was capable of more than shoving ice-cold blood through his veins. "I'm here, sweet. And you're safe. Nothing will hurt you, I promise."

*Except him,* the knowledge taunted.

Shayne's gaze followed the gentle fingers of light that traced across the impressive width of her husband's shoulders, chasing the shadows deep into the crevices of his work-hardened muscles. She couldn't see all of him. Darkness ate into their circle of privacy, concealing him from the waist down. But the lamplight fell full on his face, turning his eyes to an impossible shade of blue. It also highlighted the sharply angled cheekbones and the sun-weathered creases that told of a man who'd ridden a long, hard road.

He returned her look in full, taking his time about it. Then he clasped her wrists in one hand and lifted them over her head, anchoring them there while he studied her even more closely. Without a word, he dipped toward her, finding the jagged line that ran from wrist to the tender inner curve of her upper arm. She shuddered at the first touch of his mouth, shivering helplessly beneath each rasping lap of his tongue. Inch by torturous inch, he followed the scar until he reached the end. Only it wasn't the end.

He rolled her onto her side, her hands still shackled above her, allowing the light to fall on all of the other scars, ones only her doctors had ever seen. And then he kissed them one by one, a thousand kisses of tenderness. "How old are they?" he demanded.

"Old."

"How old? Five years?"

"Yes."

"Six?"

"Yes!"

"Or is it eight years?" He released her wrists and cupped her face, forcing her to meet the sorrow burning in his eyes. "How about eight years and one month. Could that be how old they are? You were on your way to the Montagues' Anniversary Ball, weren't you? To try and find me and start our life again."

Tears threatened, tears of regret and longing, tears of sorrow for one careless jerk of the wheel on a rain-slick mountain road. "Yes," she cried. "I'm sorry, Chaz. So sorry. I did try to get to you. I did."

He stopped her words with a kiss of such passionate poignancy that the tears flowed unchecked. "It's in the past," he said with unmistakable finality.

He found the scars with his mouth again, but instead of filling her with a shivery pleasure, they roused an unbearable tension. His hand accidentally brushed her breast. Or was it accidental? His callused fingers grazed the softness of her lower belly where there were no scars. Her muscles rippled tight. A fluttering started there, centered deep in the most feminine core of her. With each careless touch, it intensified, causing a throbbing between her legs and driving the crowns of her breasts into tight, painful peaks.

"Please," she gasped, unable to stand another minute.

"I plan to please you, sweetheart. I plan to please you every which way I can plus any others that come to mind in the next few hours."

He cupped her breasts, giving them his full attention. Her breath quickened, just as her body quickened, drawing taut with need. He lay heavily over her, slipping his hands beneath her thighs and parting them. He found the center of liquid warmth, dipped into it, intensified it, gorged on it, reveled in it. And when they were both mindless with desire, he filled her, riding with her to an ecstasy that made them inescapably one. One mind. One heart. One soul.

Joined in a perfect, shattering union.

It wasn't until much, much later, until the darkest hours of the night when nightmares roam and uncertainty cavorts, that he awoke and knew the truth. *She planned to leave him and there wasn't a damn thing he could do about it.*

"You've done *what*?"

Shayne sat up and dragged the covers around her, glaring at Chaz. "I knew you'd overreact when you found out. That's why I didn't tell you sooner."

"You listen up, wife, and you listen up good. It will be a cold day in hell before I allow that old bat to live under my roof. Do you have any idea the months of torture she's put me through?"

"She's only trying to protect Sarita."

He thrust a pillow behind his shoulders and glared at his turncoat wife. "Bull. She's trying to drive me insane."

"Sarita needs her. Besides, it's too late to tell her no. I've already said yes."

"Find a way."

"How am I supposed to do that?" she demanded in exasperation.

"Lie to her. Be honest with her. Explain that we

don't have a room for her. Frankly, I don't give a damn. But you make sure Her Worship and that cane of hers are on the next outbound transport to Mexico.''

''There's only one small problem with your plan.''

His jaw made a prominent appearance again. ''And what's that?''

''I can't tell her we don't have room because...'' She gulped. ''Because she's already seen it.''

''What do you mean, she's already seen it? Seen what?''

''I mean I...'' Her voice dropped to a barely audible level. ''I fixed up one of the bedrooms for her and let her see it.''

''You did *what*?''

She refused to take all the blame for this. ''If you'd bothered to take a look at the improvements I've been making, you'd have seen it, too. I didn't hide anything I was doing.''

He erupted from the bed. ''Are you trying to tell me you planned this from the beginning?''

''I'm not *trying* to tell you anything. I *am* telling you.''

Why was it that every time she got him naked, he left the bed angry? She cupped her chin in her hand. She must be doing something terribly wrong. Maybe if they didn't use a bed next time... His chest distracted her, rising and falling in a way she found entirely too provocative. No doubt it was deliberate.

''Let me get this straight,'' he said. ''You remodeled one of my bedrooms specifically for Doña Isabella?''

''Yes.''

''So she'd...'' He closed his eyes. ''I can hardly bring myself to say this. So she'd *stay*?''

"Yes and yes."

"Why?"

Finally. A question she could answer. "Because Sarita needs her."

"Sarita will have us."

"It's not the same, Chaz. Believe me, I know." Before he could follow up her statement with any unwanted questions, she continued. "Doña Isabella is someone your daughter's known since birth and the only family left on her mother's side. At least, the only family who'll accept her. Isabella hasn't said anything, but I suspect the reason she didn't want to take Sarita back to Mexico with her was because of the reception your daughter would have received from the rest of Madalena's family."

Dammit! He hated when Shayne was right. "I hadn't thought of that," Chaz admitted, adding stubbornly, "but that shouldn't keep Isabella from going."

"Have you any idea what it's like to be three years old and torn from the only family you've ever known?"

There was an odd quality to her voice, something that captured his attention as nothing else would have. "Of course not." He deliberately paused a beat. "Do you?"

She moistened her lips, her nervousness a dead giveaway. "Yes." She rushed into speech. "Granted, Sarita will be with people who love her. But it's not the same as being with the woman who's raised her from birth."

"This has something to do with your aunt, doesn't it? The one Rafe rescued you from."

Shayne nodded, her delicate features lined with dread. "I never talk about that time. Not even with my brother. But for Sarita…'' She closed her eyes. ''I will for Sarita's sake.''

Aw, hell. ''No, honey—''

''Rafe and I have different mothers. Did you know that?''

''You don't have to say another word,'' he tried again.

But she didn't listen. Her focus had turned inward. Even her body seemed gathered in on itself, balled tight to offer up as little surface space as possible. A horrifying thought occurred to him. It was almost as though she'd curled herself into as small a target as possible. Is that how she'd learned to protect herself as a child?

''Our father and my mother were killed in a boating accident when I was three. Rafe was just sixteen. Despite being so young, he tried to keep us together. He worked the coffee fields, ran the household, cared for me. He did everything possible to keep his family intact.''

''I had no idea,'' he said gently. He sat down next to her and drew her close, massaging the rigidness from taut muscles and offering what little comfort she'd allow.

''He lost it all, Chaz. Our home. Our money. By the end, he was desperate. He couldn't even put food on our plates.''

''What did he do?''

''Right before Christmas, he used his last penny to call my mother's sister, Jackie, and ask if she'd take me in. Jackie had never approved of my parents' marriage, but she did her duty. She flew to Costa Rica and took me back to Florida with her.''

''What about Rafe?''

Shayne's mouth twisted. "She left him behind. He wasn't her responsibility. As far as she was concerned, he was some filthy peasant child from Costa Rica, related only through an accident of marriage. For years, she wouldn't even say his name. Just that…that disgusting description."

Chaz found it difficult to reconcile the man he knew with the boy Rafe must have been. "She abandoned him?"

"I wish she'd left me, too, even if it meant living on the streets," Shayne whispered. "It would have been kinder."

Chaz stilled. "What the hell did she do to you?"

If he hadn't been holding her, he wouldn't have felt the tiny tremor that rippled through her body. "Nothing overt. Nothing that child welfare could use to remove me from the home. But I paid the price for what she regarded as my mother's sins. The first thing she did when we arrived in Florida was to burn all my possessions, including the doll Rafe had given me for a Christmas present." She attempted a smile, the tremulous pull of her lips so vulnerable and so sad, it was painful to witness. "You asked me why having a tree was so important.… I never had one the entire time I lived with her. I was the original Cinderella. Isn't that a riot? And Jackie relished the role of wicked stepmother."

Stark stories followed, ones he knew with soul-crippling certainty she'd never revealed to another person, not even Rafe. Stories that had him clutching her convulsively, helpless to protect the child she'd been. "What about your brother?" he asked, when her throat grew hoarse and the words ran dry. "He found you, didn't he?"

"Yes, he found me."

But it hadn't been in time. Not nearly in time, Chaz realized. "How old were you?"

"Thirteen."

Ten years. Forever to a helpless child. And almost as long as it had taken Chaz to find her. "So Jackie just turned you over?"

"Oh, no." Shayne looked at him then, her eyes huge, wounded smudges in her tightly drawn face. "She sold me to him."

A roar of fury welled up inside, one even more tortured than before. His throat worked as he forced it down, forced himself to offer succor for a wound that couldn't be healed. He held her in his arms and rocked her, murmuring meaningless words of comfort.

"You don't understand, Chaz. I didn't tell you this for my sake."

"Shh. Everything will be all right."

"No, it won't." She eased back and captured his face within the softness of her palms. "I know you can't love me anymore. That doesn't mean you can't love Sarita. She's an innocent child. Don't let her go through what I did. She needs Isabella just as I needed Rafe. But she needs you even more. Please, Chaz. Do this one thing for me and I won't ask you for anything else."

"Don't, Shayne."

"I'm begging you. I promise I won't cause you any more trouble."

He couldn't bear it. "Sarita doesn't have anything to worry about."

Shayne expelled her breath in a relieved sigh and Chaz closed his eyes, fighting an almost incapacitating fear. "I promise I won't cause you any more trouble," she'd claimed. She might as well have said, "I've created your home for you, here are the instructions for taking care of it."

It was a farewell, if he'd ever heard one.

He needed to swear, to vent his frustrations with a truly nasty word. He fought to come up with one, even a mild one, just something to blister the air, just a single oath to ease the confusing tumble of emotions that muddled his brain. But nothing came to him. Nothing but a single jittery warning, ringing with all the clarity of silvery bells on a winter's breeze.

*She was going to leave him.*

# CHAPTER TEN

CHAZ paused outside the door to the parlor, startled to find his foreman sitting with Doña Isabella. Now there was a sight he'd never expected to see. Neither of them noticed him, so he shoved his Stetson to the back of his head and blatantly eavesdropped.

"Now, Izzy," Penny said. "I don't want you to be upset when I put my cards down."

"I won't be the least upset."

"It's jes' that I've noticed you don't take well to losing."

"Carry on with the game, Señor Penworthy. I believe I called?"

"So you did. But, Izzy, I warned you about calling me Penworthy. If word got out that was my legally binding name, I'd be a laughingstock."

"As you wish, Señor Penny."

"That's better." He spread out his cards. "Read 'em and weep, precious. Full house, aces and kings."

"Very impressive." She stayed his hand as he reached for the pot of matchsticks with the gold-tipped handle of her cane. "But not so fast."

"You can't have my full house beat. You drew four cards!"

"Ah, but they were four excellent cards." She plunked down a fistful of queens and actually grinned. "My pot, I believe."

Chaz shook his head in disbelief. He never thought he'd live to see the day when those two would get chummy. It gave him an odd feeling. As odd as when he'd walked into the kitchen earlier. His daughter had been perched on Mojo's lap slapping balls of cookie dough onto a metal tray. She'd waved at him, her fingers studded with bits of chocolate chips, chattering at great length in a mixture of Spanish and English while Mojo sat there, not understanding a word, a big, sloppy grin on his ugly mug.

It was the same sappy expression he'd worn ever since the two had first met, the day Sarita had darted into the kitchen before anyone could stop her. Mojo had been at his worktable, frozen in place, a potato peeler poking out of his massive paw. Sarita had skidded to a halt at his side. But instead of running shrieking from the room or reacting with fear, she'd studied him with open curiosity. Then she'd climbed onto his lap, and there she'd stayed. From that moment on, they'd been the best of friends.

So why did Chaz feel so out of sorts? He should be delighted. He'd assembled all the various pieces necessary for the life he'd always wanted and Shayne had put those pieces in order. The end result was a home more perfect than he could have ever imagined.

So what the hell was bothering him?

He wandered into his office and stood by the window overlooking the front of the house. He knew what it was. Shayne and that damn Christmas tree. Shayne and the hideous childhood she'd barely survived. Shayne and her unending search for love. He suspected what hurt her the most about their relationship was that he'd let her down, first by failing to find her in the years that had passed since their marriage nine years ago. And second, and most importantly, because he didn't love her the way she so desperately needed.

*She was going to leave him.*

Now that she'd created a home for him, she'd go, and there was only one thing he could think of to stop her. He could prove that he'd done his best to find her. And he could let her know that once upon a time, he had loved her.

His next decision took no thought at all. Rifling through his desk drawer, he searched for the business card he'd tossed in there close to a month ago, a card he'd never thought he'd have occasion to use. Finding it, he punched in the series of numbers printed in the corner. The phone only rang once.

"Beaumont."

"You said to call if I ever needed help."

"McIntyre? Is that you?"

"Got it in one, big brother. I've decided to take you up on that offer." Chaz released his breath along with his pride. "I need your help."

Chaz found San Francisco cold and gray, the misty rain bringing a chill far more cutting than the fiercest winter his mountain home in Colorado could offer up. He stood outside the museum, silently cursing Rafe for forcing this out-of-the-way meeting. Couldn't he have just have sent the packet? Why all the games?

"McIntyre. Glad to see you could make it."

Chaz turned and greeted his brother-in-law with a handshake. "I don't recall you leaving me any choice."

"I didn't. There were things I wanted to say that I'd rather Shayne not overhear."

"So you dragged me all the way to San Francisco? That sister of yours must have incredible hearing."

A cool smile touched Beaumont's mouth. "There

might have been one other reason I chose this place. Come. As long as we're here, we might as well take a look around.''

Chaz struggled to hold onto his temper. Rafe had a regrettable tendency to take charge. Well, he'd let the man run things this time. Since he had the bit between his teeth it would be tough to stop him. But it would only continue until Chaz had what he'd come for. Then their ''brotherly'' relationship would screech to a halt and they could go back to a more natural mutual antagonism.

After wandering through the museum for a good fifteen minutes, Rafe paused near a huge mosaic. Reaching into his suit jacket, he removed a packet of papers and stared down at them with a dark frown. ''Would you mind telling me why you wish to give her this? Is it to drive us apart?''

Chaz took instant umbrage. ''Hell, no! Just what kind of man do you think I am?''

''My apologies. But if it isn't to drive a wedge between the two of us, then why? Why after all these years?''

''Because she needs to know that I did try and find her, that I didn't just give up on her.''

''Ah. I see. That means she's told you about her aunt.''

Chaz nodded. ''She told me.''

''Did she also tell you about her accident, that she was on her way to the Anniversary Ball—to you— when she crashed?''

Even though he already knew what had happened, hearing it stated so baldly filled Chaz with a helpless rage. He hadn't been there to protect her. Maybe if he'd tried harder to find her, the accident could have been prevented. "I know about the car wreck and the scars it left behind."

"And did she also tell you that she bought a ticket to the next Cinderella Ball, the one four years ago?"

Chaz didn't even try to conceal his astonishment. "I went to that ball. She wasn't there."

"That's because I took her ticket and attended in her place. Ella and I were married that night."

Chaz balled his hands into fists. "So you kept her from me again."

"It was wrong of me. I know that." Rafe lifted silvery-gray eyes, eyes filled with regret. "But consider this. If events had transpired differently, you wouldn't have Sarita."

"That's the only thing that keeps me from knocking your teeth down your throat."

Rafe wandered further down the corridor. "Then perhaps it isn't too late to recapture the love you once shared with my sister."

"It is too late," Chaz stated coldly. "Far too late."

"Are you sure that's not your pride talking?"

Damn the man! "I have no pride where Shayne's concerned. Otherwise, I wouldn't be standing here having this conversation. Nor would I give her those papers."

Rafe shook his head. "No, my friend. There's something more. Something you haven't told me. What is it?"

"You really want your pound of flesh, don't you?" Chaz gritted his teeth. "Fine. You'd have figured it out, eventually. I need what you're holding, Beaumont. If I don't give it to her, she'll leave me."

To his fury, Rafe actually chuckled. That did it! Brother-in-law or no, this time Chaz was going to beat the living tar out of the man. Before he could do more than cock his fist, Rafe paused in front of the mosaic and inclined his head toward it.

"It took her eight years to complete this."

Chaz glanced at the piece and then took a second look, then a third, stunned by what he saw. His arm sagged to his side. *It was him!* He stepped back so he could fully appreciate the scope of the piece. In the mosaic, he was climbing a trellis, just as he had all those years ago when he'd first met Shayne, half of him in shadow and half in light. His hand, the one caught in the light, reached toward a woman's hand— Shayne's hand. And in the background, the darkness gave way to a rainbow of color. It was truly the most beautiful piece of artwork he'd ever seen. The title of it was, "The Coming of a Forever Love"—the name impacted like a blow to the gut—and the artist was Shayne Beaumont.

Shayne Beaumont McIntyre, he wanted to shout. His wife.

Beside him, Rafe released his breath in a pitying sigh. "My poor sister. You don't even realize you still love her, do you?" He held out the papers. "If you hurt her, McIntyre, I'll make you pay."

Chaz took the packet without a word, barely noticing Rafe's departure. *You don't even realize you still love her, do you?* He shook his head. No. It wasn't possible. He hadn't felt love since... He closed his eyes, his throat moving convulsively. He hadn't felt love since he'd last held her in his arms. His eyes opened and he stared at the mosaic with desperate hunger. It was in her arms that he'd first found love, too. A forever love. Only he'd been too afraid to admit it.

He never knew how long he stood there. A minute. An hour. What finally propelled him into motion was an odd feeling deep in his chest. A…burgeoning. He'd told Shayne that he'd died inside years ago, but that wasn't true. Instead, those emotions had lain dormant, waiting for the return of spring. And she'd come, wearing a bell-draped mask, a tender smile and velvety eyes filled with a love so generous and so absolute that it brought humbling tears to his eyes.

His jaw worked as he forced himself to face the soul-stripping truth. He loved her. He had the first time he'd set eyes on her over nine years ago and he'd continued to right up until this very second. And he would for the rest of his life. There'd been only one thing that had kept him from admitting it.

Fear. Fear that he'd lose her again at some point in the future. Fear that he couldn't handle it if anything happened to her. But most of all, fear that she wouldn't love him as utterly as he loved her. Well, the proof of her enduring love was before his eyes, an eight-year labor of love.

He tucked the packet Rafe had given him into his coat pocket. *Well, you love-crazed fool,* he muttered to himself, *what the hell are you doing standing here?* Tomorrow was Christmas Eve and he had a home and a daughter, a grandmother and a handful of crazy employees to get back to. But most important of all, he had a wife who loved him. A wife he loved with all of his newly discovered heart.

"What's he doing?" Shayne demanded in an undertone.

Jumbo shook his head morosely. "Doin' what he

always does on Christmas Eve. He's holed up in there
with a bottle and a stack of writing papers.''

"But *why*?"

"Can't say, missy. Now why don't you get along
to the kitchen? I'm sure Mojo can find something to
keep you busy.''

She shook her head. "No, thanks, Jumbo. I don't
feel like burning anything right now.''

"Well, maybe you'll be in the mood a little later.''

Staggering her with a gentle pat on the back, Jumbo
lumbered on his way. Desperate for something to oc-
cupy her, Shayne pretended to buff the mosaic pieces
set into the floor along the hall, but really she used it
as an excuse to hang around outside Chaz's office
door. After another ten minutes of halfhearted polish-
ing, she glanced around, assuring herself that the corridor remained empty. Then she tiptoed to his door
and pressed her ear to the wood. She couldn't hear a
sound. If he sat in there drinking himself into a stupor,
he was being darned quiet about it.

"Somethin' I can help you with, little lady?''

Shayne whipped around, blushing at the amused
twinkle in Penny's eyes. "Oh, no. I was just...
Just...''

"Waxing the door with your ear?''

She sighed. "Something like that.''

"Well, then. Carry on. But you should know.'' The
laughter died from Penny's eyes. "He won't be out
until morning. Never is.''

"Oh.''

Shayne gave the door a final forlorn look before
slipping away to her bedroom. She had a few last-
minute presents to wrap, even though Christmas promised to be decidedly strange this year. Still, she

couldn't allow Sarita to be affected. She just hoped a box brimming with hair ribbons and combs and barrettes would be enough. And then there was her gift for Chaz. She sniffed, distressed to find herself in tears yet again.

Topping the small box with a colorful bow, she pushed it aside. Darn it all! Curling up on the bed, she allowed herself a good cry, hoping to get it out of her system. She was being foolish, she knew that. But tomorrow would mark the end of any chance to win Chaz's love. Once he opened her gift, her dreams for being loved for herself would end.

Surely that deserved a few tears, didn't it?

"Keep your voices down, dammit!"

"You try and wrestle a tree this big into a room half its size and see if you don't give a yelp or two," Penny complained.

Chaz gave the base of the tree a tremendous shove, sending his foreman tumbling into his office. "If you wake up my daughter or my wife, yelping is the least you'll be doing."

"Where do you want it, boss man?" Mojo asked.

"By the window." Shayne had haunted that spot for the past week. "Is the tree stand ready?"

"I've got it." Jumbo got down on his hands and knees. "Bring 'er on over. That's right. Stand her on up. No, no! More to the left. Forward. Now toward the back."

Chaz gritted his teeth. "Jumbo, if you don't get the trunk into the stand in the next three seconds, I'm gonna stick you in that thing and hang ornaments from your ears!"

"There he goes with those ears again. Somehow,

Jumbo, I don't think it's your ears he's gonna decorate."

Penny hooted. "You got that right."

"What part of 'be quiet' don't you three understand?" Chaz demanded, heaving the tree into position.

"Still can't believe you're sober enough to put up a tree, boss. What happened to your date with Jack Daniels?"

"JD and I have had a parting of the ways."

Penny grimaced. "I knew marriage would ruin you."

Chaz just grinned. "And you were right." He stood back and eyed the tree. It wasn't too crooked. Maybe if he lopped off a few branches nobody would notice the slight starboard list. "Thanks for your help. I'll take it from here."

"You don't want us to help put silly little doodads on it?" Penny grumbled.

It didn't take any thought at all. Chaz shook his head decisively. "Nope. That's my job." Actually, it was more than that. "It's my pleasure."

Shayne awoke early the next morning and rolled over, knowing before she even looked that she wouldn't find her husband beside her. Quietly, she left the bed and pulled on a robe. She needed to talk to him before anyone else in the household stirred. It was Christmas morning and she had to find a way to make him understand the importance of the day to a small child, something she'd obviously failed to do so far.

She slipped through the silent house, heading straight for Chaz's office. The door stood ajar and she gave it a little push. Hovering there, she could only stand and stare. Her husband was sprawled on the floor, sound asleep. At the sound of her gasp, he pried open an eye, wincing at the bright sunlight filtering into the room. He muttered something beneath his breath, something she tactfully pretended not to hear.

"Oh, Chaz," she murmured. "What have you done to yourself?"

"'Mornin', sweetheart. Merry Christmas."

She blinked, not quite certain she'd heard him right. "You know what day it is?"

"Of course I know." His eyes were red-rimmed, but alert, his smile as devastating as ever. If he'd indulged last night, it had been with something other than a bottle of bourbon. "Don't you?"

"Well, yes, but—" She walked further into the office and then she saw it. A huge tree filled one entire end of the room. She stared at it in disbelief. "That...that looks like a Christmas tree."

Chaz folded his arms behind his head, still sprawled on the floor. "Naw. That can't be. I don't do Christmas, remember?"

She took a step closer and fingered one of the needled branches. "It feels like a Christmas tree," she said unevenly.

His brow wrinkled into a frown. "Well, I'll be. Now isn't that the strangest thing."

She released the branch and it swayed ever so slightly. An excited chorus of silver-toned bells filled the air, ringing out a happy greeting. They were the bells from her mask, she realized, tears flooding her eyes. He'd strung them, one by one, on the tree. "It—" She swallowed and tried again. "It even sounds like a Christmas tree."

"Well, heck. Then it must be one. Don't know how

the silly thing found its way in. Guess I'll have to drag it on out of here before anyone sees it."

The tears that had become such a natural part of her day overflowed her eyes. "You even decorated it."

In addition to the bells, he'd taken green and red ribbons—the colors made her cry all the harder—and tied them on the ends of each branch. The fact that the bows were a bit lopsided and imperfectly tied endeared them to her all the more.

"Honey?" He sat up. "You aren't crying, are you?"

"No," she sobbed. "I'm not."

He was on his feet in a flash. Crossing to her side in two swift strides, he pulled her into his arms. "Please don't cry, sweetheart. I did this to make you happy. Not to upset you."

"I'm not upset," she wailed.

"You sure sound upset." He bent at the knees so their height matched and peered at her face. "And if all that stuff comin' out of your eyes is any indication, you look upset, too."

"Don't you know anything?" She wrapped her arms around his waist, pressing her lips to his chest. "This is my happy face."

He smiled at that, his tension slowly easing. "Now there's a scary thought." And then he kissed her, kissed her with a passion she couldn't mistake. It was a touch that spoke of love and forever and permanence and commitment, words that were once forbidden, but now seemed imperative. "Merry Christmas, wife."

It took Shayne several minutes to recover, her lids lifting reluctantly. "I don't understand a bit of this. You put up a tree and decorated it."

"So I did."

"You must have worked on it all night."

"Just about."

She could scarcely take it in. "But...why?"

"Because I was wrong. Dead wrong. You and Sarita deserve a proper Christmas."

"You even have presents." She was dreaming, she had to be. But it appeared real, beautifully, incredibly real.

"They're nothing much." The wicked light that appeared in his eyes instantly alerted her.

"What have you done?"

"Now, honey. If I told, it wouldn't be a surprise."

Before she could ask any more questions, they heard the patter of feet outside the door. A moment later, Sarita burst into the room. Spying the tree and presents, she released a squeal of delight and threw herself into her father's arms. Chaz closed his eyes, clutching her close, the expression on his face almost painful to witness.

Then he tossed her into the air, laughing at her helpless giggles. "Merry Christmas, princess."

Mojo and Jumbo plowed through the doorway next, with Penny and Doña Isabella not far behind. "Check the tree! Not bad, boss man."

The next few hours were the most pleasurable Shayne could remember in a very long time. After changing and grabbing a quick breakfast, everyone gathered in Chaz's office to open presents. It was that day that Sarita solidified her relationship with her new parents, racing back and forth between Shayne and Chaz, dispensing hugs and kisses with such utter generosity that if Shayne hadn't already fallen in love with her brand-new daughter, she'd have tumbled head over heels that day. And Chaz's expression was filled with such an abiding joy that tears were never far from the surface.

Doña Isabella and Chaz's men were also the recipient of Sarita's affections as she darted from one to the other as they each opened their presents. She oohed and aahed over everything, no matter how ridiculous, from the meat cleaver for Mojo, "since he has a tendency to throw his away," to the first-class clipboard that turned Jumbo pale with fright. Chaz didn't spare any of his employees from his warped sense of humor. For Penny, he'd wrapped up a huge box of matchsticks and a deck of marked playing cards. "So you can win a few." And when Shayne dared to scold him, he'd simply laughed and whispered that he'd also put a fat bonus in their paychecks, a surprise they'd appreciate far more than any other gift he could have chosen.

He'd kept his present for Doña Isabella more serious, giving her a beautiful quilted dressing gown and cozy slippers. Shayne had drawn a sketch of the mosaic patio she'd build for Isabella come spring. And Sarita took one look at the fancy new dollhouse her daddy had brought back from San Francisco and disappeared into the corner, happily playing. She only emerged on those occasions she wanted her new "momma" to change her hair ribbons, rhapsodizing over the many choices.

At long last, Chaz drew Shayne away from the others, a small, flat box in his hand. "I'd rather do this next part in private," he said.

She glanced around the room. Everyone was preoccupied and wouldn't miss her if she slipped off with Chaz for a while. Tucking her hand into his, she drew him toward their bedroom. "Is this private enough?" she asked.

His smile felt as tender and loving as a kiss. "This is perfect."

"So who goes first?"

"Open mine." He handed her the box.

She could see a hint of uncertainty dimming the blue of his eyes and lines of tension bracketing his mouth. He didn't know how she'd react to his gift, she realized. She stared at the box for a long moment before she carefully unwrapped it. Removing the lid, she found a stack of letters.

Her brow furrowing, she lifted out the first one. Her name was scrawled across the envelope and it had been sent care of the Montagues. And then she saw the date. Christmas Eve, nine years ago. Slowly she turned over the envelope. It was sealed.

"Open it," he said.

Without a word she removed the letter and read it. And then she reached for the next, dated Christmas Eve, a year later. And then the next, until she'd read his testament to a decade of enduring love.

The final one wasn't postmarked. "You…you wrote this last night, didn't you?" she asked unevenly. "When you were locked up in your office with Jack."

"No Jack Daniels. Just a stack of writing paper and a pen. It takes me a while to get the letters right. Most of the night, usually. But for some strange reason, I found this one a lot easier. Which left plenty of time for a few other chores."

He meant the tree and decorations, she realized. As she had with all the others, she turned the envelope over and pried it open, removing the single sheet of paper with hands that trembled. Sure enough, it bore yesterday's date.

> *To My Newly Found Bride,*
> *There's only one thing left to say. Only one thing I've neglected to say. Only one thing that would have been said if I hadn't been so afraid.*
> *I love you.*
> *My wife. My one true love. My Forever Love.*

By the time she'd finished reading, she was so overcome with emotion, she couldn't speak. "There's one last item," he said. "It's in the bottom of the box."

Barely able to see through her tears, she pulled aside the tissue paper. Two golden tickets glittered in the subdued lighting. Tickets to next year's Anniversary Ball. "Oh, Chaz," she whispered.

"I know it's ten months away, but I thought maybe we could make it a date. Right now."

"I don't understand." She stared at him in bewilderment. "You were so sure you couldn't love anyone."

"I was wrong. I loved you from the first moment I set eyes on you. I've always loved you. Fear held me back." His mouth tightened. "I never thought of myself as a coward. But denying how I felt for you was easier than facing the truth. Safer than admitting that without you I was only living half a life. And I was furious, Shayne. Down to the bones, raw with anger. Angry at your brother for parting us. Angry at you for not coming back to me. Mostly, angry at myself for not finding you."

She offered a look of utter understanding. "I know all about fear and anger, remember?"

He met her gaze then, straight and earnest and totally frank. "I love you, Shayne. I always have and I always will. I'm sorry it's taken me so long to come to my senses."

She slipped into his arms and kissed him, a kiss of love and forgiveness. A kiss of promise. A kiss of passion. When they drew apart, she handed him the present she'd wrapped for him. "I don't know how you'll take to this," she confessed.

"I'm sure I'll love it, whatever it is." He used far less care than she had opening the box. He ripped the paper away and pulled off the top. And then he simply sat, not uttering a word.

She regarded him apprehensively. "Aren't you going to say something?"

He picked up the baby rattle. "You're pregnant? For real?"

She nodded. "For real."

Without a word, he tipped her backward onto the bed and pushed up her sweater, baring her stomach and cupping the slight swell with gentle hands. "This—" He blinked hard. "This is the best present you could have given me."

"Are you sure?"

A blissful smile touched his mouth. "Oh, yeah, sweetheart. I'm real sure." Then he frowned. "There's only one problem."

"What's that?" she asked nervously.

"You don't suppose..." He broke off and shook his head. "Naw. It's too ridiculous."

"What?"

"I just had this terrible thought."

*"Chaz!"*

He slanted her a teasing glance. "You don't suppose this means Mojo really does have the eye, do you?''

She chuckled. ''I'll tell you how we'll know for sure.''

''Yeah? How's that.''

She sat up and wrapped her arms around his neck. ''We'll know for sure if he 'sees' our next baby before Mother Nature confirms it.''

''Our *next* baby? You mean the one after this?''

''That's generally what 'next' means.''

Laughter rumbled through Chaz's chest, a happy, contented sound. ''Okay. You're on.''

# EPILOGUE

SHAYNE sat curled up in the leather chair behind Chaz's desk and grinned at her husband, blinking a suspicious moisture from her eyes. He lay on the floor in front of the Christmas tree, overwhelmed by a flurry of pigtails and giggles. Even Sarita, so grown up at eight years, wasn't too big to wrestle her daddy to the ground. And she was such a loving big sister to Caitlin and the babies—twin girls that Mojo had "seen" long before the doctors. Despite his original terror at the notion, Chaz had gotten his house full of girls, after all.

The past five years had been the best of Shayne's life, years of love and laughter and incomparable joy. Years of richness with Chaz and the girls, Isabella and Mojo and Jumbo and Penny. Her youngest toddled over to her, looking for her mother's lap, and Shayne was only too happy to accommodate.

Nibbling the end of her pen, she returned to her yearly letter. By Christmas morning, Chaz would find the envelope hidden somewhere on the tree, a tradition that had started on their first anniversary. She didn't doubt it was a tradition that would continue for the rest of their lives. Cuddling her daughter close, she rested her cheek against the silky curls and put pen to paper.

*To My Forever Love*...she began.

# *Harlequin Romance*®

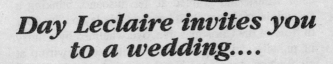

FAIRYTALE WEDDINGS

## *Day Leclaire invites you to a wedding....*

On one magical night, single people attend a glittering, masked Wedding Ball with one purpose in mind: to meet and marry their perfect partner! The idea is blissfully simple: Come single, leave wed!

### Look out for:
### November 1999
### #3575 BRIDEGROOM ON APPROVAL
### and
### December 1999
### #3579 LONG-LOST BRIDE

*Available at your favorite retail outlet.*

# HARLEQUIN®
*Makes any time special.*™

Visit us at: www.romance.net                    HRFW